Flying Elbows

Also by Ernest Lockridge

ERNEST LOCKRIDGE

Flying Elbows

STEIN AND DAY/*Publishers*/New York

First published in 1975
Copyright © 1975 by Ernest Lockridge
All rights reserved
Designed by Ed Kaplin
Printed in the United States of America
Stein and Day/*Publishers*/Scarborough House,
Briarcliff Manor, N.Y. 10510

Library of Congress Cataloging in Publication Data

Lockridge, Ernest, 1938-
   Flying elbows.

    I. Title.
PZ4.L819Fl   [PS3562.027]   813'.5'4   75-8857
ISBN 0-8128-1812-1

For Laurel, Ellen, Sarah

Flying Elbows

CHAPTER 1

I'll warn you now, I've lied during my life. When you confess the truth, you never know what names you'll win, like in high school when I told the first so-called nice boy I ever went out with what'd been done to me, letting myself go like a dumb kid. With his mouth gaping wide enough to swallow me whole, pounding the steering wheel of his daddy's Buick Eight, he yelled, "Liar! Liar!" then knuckled down to hollering, "Lowdown whore," whining he hadn't believed his friends, but now he knew I'd earned every word they told him, and Lord knew what was going to befall his golden reputation. Poor child. That was right before his old man, the flying dentist, landed in the slammer for cheating Uncle Sam blind. And if they'd made me testify in court, I could've nailed him for another crime—he wouldn't have flown free after only one year, and got reelected country club president. And his son's jaw would have unhinged itself like a snake's, and their whole life would have blown apart ten times more. No matter how much crud a person confesses, there's worse coiled up right behind. You're better off not asking.

I don't hold grudges and don't want to hurt another person's feelings. But now I'm partly well educated, and by scribbling the past few months on paper maybe like Joy Silverspring I can make money off my life, and so tidy it up, like stitching a wound, letting the clean scar give me comfort. Maybe I can even sell this to the flicks, since the time from September to Christmas Day of last year promises to be a real Oscar-winner.

Not that I'm griping. I've had my share of saviors. And ripping through your day like a wildwoman sure beats hatching your rear before *Love of Life*—if you don't get killed. As a kid, seeing news pictures that looked like adventure, I'd say, "I want to ride that horse!" "I want to fly that plane!" "I want to climb that mountain!" "Live in that mansion!" "Blow that bridge sky-high!" Little Casey wasn't blitzing my wavelength then, neither were the Treasure House, Billy Graham, Sergeant Bill Wilson, Brother DeProspo, and the Cat Burglar. I've helped crack a bushel of eggs, I guess. But I never have been a person to rail over Humpty Dumpty.

Sometimes I think that all I ever wanted was life, liberty, and enough property to buy me peace of mind. Is that so damned awful?

One morning last September, among ten bills I found two letters, which I tore open and read outside on my porch. One, marked Postage Due from Jasper, Indiana, bloomed like barbed wire in old Ethel's messy scrawl, though there wasn't any handwriting, neatest or fanciest, she couldn't duplicate. She had a healthy string of arrests for forgery and counterfeiting, but had been cagey enough to serve less than three years in her whole ornery life.

"Baby Daughter," she wrote, "that bastard Charlie caught me redhanded at what I shouldn't of been doin, ha ha, and is kickin me out nekkid. Should of knowed it wd crack up one day, dumbass Charlie having the coldest rear end of any bum made by God. Of course, Amelia, there is another. But he only got enough for your old Mom's busfare so I can hide with you til this divorcing is dead and buried. How come the world treats me like dirt? All I know is, God must want me awful bad to see my last grandchild before I die.

"Hugs and smacks from your own

Mom
"P.S. You don't know Buster, but he's a peach."

Truth was, I didn't even know Charlie. Standing in housecoat and slippers on the front porch, I wondered what he or any other peach saw in a fifty-eight-year-old two-hundred-pound tubful of fifty different breeds of bug, front crisscrossed with scars and puckers from a dozen operations, one leaving a long pink slicemark where her bellybutton was. Some peaches will stuff anything that holds still, I guess.

The second letter, thick and broad, came from the Indiana Pen. "Hi there Sweetheart," Lonzo wrote in his big, sloppy, cheerful scribble. "Your ramblin, gamblin man has had a scrape or two and has landed here on Cloud Nine, otherwise known as the State Slammer. But don't worry about a thing. I've got the hang of the joint. Biggest fret is to hold queers in this fruithouse from splitting my backside. Ha ha. But about all I can think of these days is you, you big gorgeous hunk of woman, and my own two little girls, and even poor little Jenny who you somehow got by your faggot other husband Errol Shiflet. If you want the truth, I blame that burnt-out fishloving fart for all the horseshit our second time around. Don't know why in hell you wanted to get educated, when in my eyes you always was a good low-class woman. Probly pisses you off, don't it.

"Well, I sure have been living like one fool. First thing since that last money order you got, I'm in this Naptown bar, white bar I think, but two shines crowd on both my sides and there wasn't nobody else in the place, and one boogie says, 'White boys is half man,' and I hadn't said *nothin*, but grunt when they sit, like I was disgusted. And the other says, so I smell his breath, 'Gal tol me honkeys ain't even got that,' so I says, 'You pinheads want to see who's a man, let's us step in the gents for show and tell.' Whew! Hitting four or five honkeytonks must of queered my brains, because them guys usually give me the willies, because in the gents they pull shivs, and one says, low and filthy, 'Motherfuck, you recall whose wheels you smashed into outside?' So help me, I couldn't recall nothing. Next thing, I wake up, stitched like a baseball in a hospital bed, and this deputy looking down at me like his eyes was steel.

"But that ain't half. I'm on the street after being in court, job in Rod's Fine Cars lost, and the judge telling *me*, though I ain't but got cut, if I don't pump ship he'd have me canned in jig time, when this fullgrowed woman, way over the hill for a hooker, rubs my ass in The Velvet Drum and says, would I like a little fun, and you know I been a funlover all my life, and remember, kid, you divorced *me* both times, not the other way round, and I no more than get washed off in her room when the fuzz bust in and cuff me for statutory. 'Hell!' I hollered. 'That little girl's somebody's Granma!'

"But the court said she was fourteen, and I'm doin one to ten. That's U.S. justice, though Lord knows I'm a Joe Palooka patriot. Have you still got that little keepsake by the sack for luck?

"So this is why the alimony is all dried up, which I never did begrudge a cent of, and why I ain't makin that visit I once promised you and the kiddies. But the other point is this, honey, though your probly wonderin what in heck to make of a old galoot like me and want to ring my neck like a rooster, I ain't got nobody else to help me out of here and one to ten sure pokes out ahead, and there ain't but black boys in this place. If anything gives me willies, it's gettin cornholed by a queer boogie. Ain't even got my guitar. Maybe could you scrape up something and find some hotshot shyster to spring a innocent man so he can come home to his kiddies and ex-wife for Christmas? Then me and you'll get back together, cause through thick and thin it always did seem like we was made for each other. Surely you do know how sorely your missed, believe you me I dream of your pretty smiling face hauling mé out of this here sinkhole. Then you can reap the full measure of thankyvoos from your

Lonzo Biggs"

CHAPTER 2

To keep things straight, the Pen's censor had a generous go at Lonzo's letter, heavy black stampmarks like belts across the middle of his tall words, so I had to make up part of what you've just read. If you didn't throw up halfway through.

But I knew Lonzo well, and as you can tell he was one prize. My pretty face reaching down to haul him out—by the teeth? Oh, Lonzo, you hill ape! If the dope was going to die, it'd be over his peter, sticking it out like a gooseneck—to have it whacked in half. And whatever Errol's considerable faults, he wasn't a faggot. Though like all men he foamed with such nonsense as, "Hey, know about Randolph Scott? He's a roaring fairy." Sure. So are Joe Louis, James Dean, Godzilla, Jesus Christ, and God the Father if it makes you feel better to think so.

"Probly pisses you off." What? Calling me low-class? Sure those blacks cut him for nothing. I see Lonzo smashing their car against a post, flashing the finger, and peeling out blasting gravel. And that little girl was really ten, I bet, and Lonzo thought he'd stuck his claws into an eight-year-old. Anybody who exposes himself without meaning to should be kept from touching pencil to paper.

But then Lonzo had his good points. He was a natural lover, never trying strange tricks like Errol Shiflet, Ph.D., who'd learned too much in a shut closet and had his mind

tossed off the track, or maybe was just imitating his perverted father. And Lonzo didn't begrudge the alimony. He
could stop paying, move in next door, and I'd never set the
law on him. One hundred ninety bucks a month is hard for a
man who can't keep a job four weeks, though he probably
stole half and sent it out of guilt for that bug-ridden harlot
Lillian Jones I divorced him over the second time round.

I thought about the women he screwed before they
canned him, a shame, really, sticking all that energy in a
cage, except it never led to any good. Then I recalled how
we'd raise hell together, how fun it was, though I'm no
criminal and knew it was wrong. And thinking of Lonzo
screwing and having one good old time while I was stuck
with three kids, though I love them, pinching pennies,
studying, going to school two evenings a week, staying
awake half the night wondering where the next buck to feed
my daughters is coming from, and Ethel, the old packrat,
threatening to show in however long it takes a Greyhound
from Indiana to Connecticut, to gulp grub—thinking about
these tough knots made me so mad, I found myself whacking
my palm against the house.

"Mamma, why can't you behave yourself? Some man in a
black suit just walked by and saw you throwing a tantrum."
Marlene, my oldest, stood in the door. Her long blond hair
stuck out in all directions like a frizzy haystack, and she wore
a purple skirt that barely packaged her crotch.

"You must be afraid I'll spoil business," I shot back.
"First thing this evening, I'll screw your red porchlight in."

"Mamma dear," Marlene drawled, "we don't do things
like when you were a little girl. Hadn't you heard? It's all
handled by phone. Otherwise, I'm just following in your
footsteps."

Since Marlene turned sixteen, I never had been able to
get anything past her. But so long as she was quick with a
comeback, she couldn't be lousing up her brain with drugs.

Marlene patted my shoulder. "Really, what's wrong,
Mamma?"

Lord, who would get us through tomorrow, I was wondering, let alone the whole month? Even Ethel, that huge bladderful of pus and snot, could always dredge up a thing in pants, change in its pocket. I don't know. Though Marlene was ten times smarter than me, I wasn't about to make her my mother, the way Ethel did me before I was ten. "Honey, wake up," she'd say. "Honey, I done caught crabs from some gent whose name I can't recall. What am I gonna do now?" I'd made enough mess of Marlene's life without upsetting nature.

So I didn't answer right off, noticing the sunny air that smelled so clean and wet. At the curb, dew still fogged the windows of the old '57 Chevy, sturdy as a Patton tank, which Lonzo left me when last he passed through.

"Grandma's coming," I finally said, heading back inside.

"Which one?" Marlene asked.

"Ethel."

"Oh boy, Grandma Dollarhide eats like a sow. But Errol's mom is the one I can't stand. Last time I saw that old bat with her dyed red hair, she wanted to know, did I take dope, and did I have my cherry?" This must have been the year before when Dr. and Mrs. Shiflet had spent the whole month visiting good friends of theirs in Orange, near the Maltby Lakes, six miles from where we lived. "Know what I told her?" Marlene said.

"I don't want to."

"That I'd still be a virgin if Errol Shiflet, Ph.D., hadn't raped me every night those years he pretended to be my father. Told her he didn't do much damage, because she'd sure given birth to a crummy lay." Marlene looked wildly pleased with herself. I felt like a hot Coke needing its cap snapped off.

"The worst thing a girl your age can have," I said, "is a bad reputation."

"Mamma, I was kidding."

"Wouldn't put anything past Errol Shiflet," I muttered. "With those parents, it's a wonder he isn't a mass murderer like that Richard Speck."

"I can't even crack a joke!" Marlene stalked ahead of me

into the bright kitchen, where Jenny and little Bess waited in their school clothes for breakfast. This crazy image filled my mind, that my family was a children sandwich, Errol's one daughter stuck between a pair of Lonzo's, and suddenly I felt so helpless to save my girls that I couldn't walk ten feet to the fridge to give them food. It was as if something had gone dead wrong with my life years back, but I couldn't remember what it was, and so it kept festering and rotting till now it was almost too far gone to heal.

"Mommy, I drawed this picture." Bess, five then, waved a sheet of yellow paper up from the table.

"Drew," I said. "Low-class people say drawed."

"Among other low-class actions," Marlene sassed.

The picture looked like three walleyed monsters attacked by scribble marks. "That's a queen in the middle of a mommy and a daddy," Bess said. "They're crying, because all the poison perfume is coming in and they're afraid to be killed."

"She sure does have some imagination," Jenny said slowly, as if each syllable had to be fired off by a separate thought. Jenny was twelve, and so fat it broke my heart.

"That was my dream," Bess went on. "It's why I peepeed my bed."

"It's the truth, Mother." Jenny slept upstairs with Bess. "We were hoping you wouldn't find out until after we got off to school."

Bess went to kindergarten in the McChesney Binford Grade School, a block away. Marlene and Jenny went another half mile after walking her there, to Malcolm X, on the river, cattails and water reeds sprouting ten feet high beside the schoolgrounds. You didn't dare pass the place at night, even though a big monastery stood right next door, because rapists, perverts, and muggers crouched by the water, spiders in an old closet. The monastery was only three years old, and looked like a Holiday Inn.

My fridge, when I finally pulled it open, showed two eggs, cracked and leaking, an inch of milk, a brown cabbage, one half lemon, dry and puckered, a white dish covered for

16

two months with wax paper, a hunk of naked cheese, solid as stone, six slices of Wonder Bread, a withered apple, and a smell like the butch matron's breath at my reform school.

"Somebody should have gone to Champion's market," Marlene said.

"I want Cocoa Wheats," Bess cried out.

But I wailed, "It's too darn much!" and ran through the pantry and dining room to the bare stairs. In the girls' rooms, clothes heaped the cold floors. Sheets I hadn't changed for weeks dangled like monster tongues off beds. And I imagined all that dirt and pee might bring the whole smelly mess to life, like a comic book I read as a kid where some man murdered his mother, then buried her in his basement under oily rags, dead canaries and goldfish, which slowly grew into a warm blob of slime. One night the man forgot to look where he was going, and the blob simply swallowed him.

In my room, where black cracks spanned the walls and ceiling, I buried my head under the covers till at last the girls banged out.

CHAPTER 3

Then I said to myself, "Amelia, get back in control." My hand still clutched the wad of bills, and sitting on the mattress, I opened them, plus a few others that I'd stuck away in the nightstand, where the upstairs phone sat. My friend Joy Silverspring said her childhood was so joyous and uneventful she couldn't remember anything before she was twelve years old, which was probably why she seemed so happy as a grown-up. But I remember most everything, especially crap. This made Errol jealous, though you might as well envy an attic crammed with dust.

Water was $24.90, due in one week or they'd shut me off; electric, $36.72 for a single month because the girls never turn off their damn lights; car insurance, $196, a jump of $100 because Marlene had gotten her driver's license in August; luckily I'd managed to scrape together the premium for my homeowner's policy two months earlier. Phone, $67.85, two months past due, and a red sticker on the bill saying they'd shut off service in two days; my bank bounced two checks, a $5 penalty; mortgage, $125, not bad considering the large house. Errol's dad had staked us a small down payment thirteen years before, certainly to buy off his guilt for almost murdering his own son. Dr. Burke, horny daddy-o who chewed a stogie even when he poked your privates, billed me $46, harking back six months when Marlene was having terrible cramps. Luckily we're a healthy family by and large, and Dr. Burke only charged peanuts per office visit, because he's such a notorious oddball. The dentist's bill was $167, because of poor Jenny's teeth. The new Macy's, my only charge account—they sent half of Elm City credit cards when they opened—wanted a total of $515.58, including $64.99 in new purchases and $6.97 interest for one month or a minimum of $80 on the revolving payment plan, four months past due. If I didn't send the $80, I'd have, they said, to pay the whole balance. They might as well dun me a million. I'd flown that little plastic wafer like a magic carpet, but what did they expect, pouring honey on a fly? The most scary bill came from Gorgeous George, my grocer—$177.52, and in his big snotty scrawl this threat: "No more credit until Mrs. Shiflet-Biggs pays what is owed."

Listing these amounts on the back of the phone company's envelope, I enjoyed neatness and order the first time that morning, till I figured what I owed: $925.99 if I sent Macy $80, $1,365.75 if I had to pay it all. If I didn't come up with $637.99 on the Q.T., we wouldn't be allowed to eat, see after dark, drink water, phone, drive a car, or live indoors. During cold weather, oil in our big drafty house cost $100 per month. You had to pay. I pulled the checkbook out of the nightstand. An uncertain $3.76 left. I never troubled to balance the thing. In two weeks, welfare would hawk up $85, one gob of spit in a sewer, like the measly $65 Errol chipped in each month for Jenny, though Lord knows the poor child had to stop eating and digest some blubber off herself. Night school tuition at Elm City University had hit me hard, $300 for one American lit course, taught by this jittery bearded boy who often stuttered out the opposite of what he meant, so I had to listen hard. He'd also announce, "There are three reasons," start wandering on the second, and forget he'd ever mentioned any third.

I wondered how my life had drifted so far beyond control. Like Bess, I'd been having creepy dreams of late, though they hadn't yet made me wet the bed. In a dream I had more than once, it was winter and I stood on the frozen surface of the quarry I swam in as a kid. I had to walk gingerly, because the ice was thin as eggshell, and from underneath in the water, someone whispered, "World's deepest, world's deepest." With a quiet pop, the ice broke, like I'd stuck my foot through Saran Wrap. Falling, I tried to remember where and who I was, as a clammy flipper touched inside my thigh and burst my eyes awake.

Maybe I was heading into my Change of Life, and that was screwing up my mind. But I was thirty-four, and strong, with only enough soft flesh to make me curve, my white teeth without one hole, and my hair a prettier blond than Marlene's, though if I kept worrying it'd snow up fast. I didn't smoke, and hardly ever drank, and knew that if Marlene and I ever went out on the street, it'd be nip and tuck which of us made more money. So I snapped up the blinds, and got down to the business of rubbing gunk around my eyesockets, to keep the crows away.

A tiny jar of eye cream cost $7.50 and curved up at the bottom, so you mostly paid for glass, and that morning I ran out, fingertip skating against the greasy whiteness. I'd forgotten to wash my face before starting, so even that tad was wasted. Maybe my brain was exploding, the way Errol Shiflet kept worrying about his, because he swilled whiskey the way a nightcrawler eats dirt. "Know what this is doing to me?" he'd ask, grinning like a fool into his huge martini. "Murdering five thousand brain cells at one whack. This shit'll make me a moron when I'm fifty. But know what's worse? The syph your whore mother passed on to you. Eating through your nervous system like a platoon of maggots!" As if I hadn't already had two negative Wassermanns, that idiot, with his aquariums full of man-eating tropical fish. And I left Lonzo for Errol because I admired a man so well educated that while we were courting he would call me things like his "beating heart of nature, his lioness, his shark-hearted goddess," and other nonsense.

Anyway, something was wrong. Looking in the mirror, I saw a red vein slash through the white of one eye. Age was catching up, my body rotting like Ethel's. Last time I'd seen Ethel, her eyeballs had almost melted in the sockets. And I was out of medicine to slow my rot, which made me angry enough to start up stealing again.

To settle myself, I recalled my moneybags dream, a good dream I'd once had after reading in the newspaper that a black man had found in the gutter a gunnysack full of real greenbacks, which had flopped out the back of an armored car. He returned the sack like a good Boy Scout, and the bank said thank you with a small reward. But the man's friends called him a fool, and hoodlums pitched bricks through his windows and set fire to his house. Sometimes honesty seems worse than murder. I remember getting all riled, too, and thinking, luck that big comes from the sky, and tossing it away is pissing in God's hand. If I believed in God.

In my dream, I found the bag, heavy, warm and leathery, lying before my house. Next, I was on my kitchen floor, spreading the bag's puckered top, plunging in with both arms to my shoulders, feeling hot, slimy money, like compost. Kneeling, I stuck my head in. A watery glow showed fives and tens in heaps, and also mashed potatoes piled up, with lakes of brown gravy where a ladle had pressed its shape. "Praise be," I murmured, filling my tummy till it almost popped.

Suddenly the phone on my nightstand clanged like the devil's pitchfork striking bone.

CHAPTER 4

"Mrs. Biggs? This is Becky Willett, your service representative at Southern New England Bell."

"Hello, honey," I said. "How are you this morning?" Because when I first picked up the phone, I heard her sigh, or moan.

A little pause while she thought that one over. "Why, fine, I guess."

"Myself, I'm feeling kind of peaked."

"What's that?" she asked.

"Hoosier for sickly."

"But I'm just fine. Mrs. Biggs?"

"Amelia," I said.

"Mrs. Biggs, sometimes my supervisor listens in like a Father Confessor."

"You sound like a Catholic, honey. Listens to what?"

"To this. Your bill to date is $67.85. We have sent you repeated notices. You must come to our downtown office by noon today and pay in full. Otherwise we must shut you off. To resume service you must pay the balance in full, plus a deposit of $90. Any questions?"

"Honey, what about the dirty phone call I got last night?" I asked.

"Well"—and I heard her giggle—"if we shut you off, you won't have to worry about getting another."

"Hey, that's good."

"It really isn't a joke. Those nuts almost always know who you are. Like if your picture's in the paper. Lots of times they live right in your neighborhood." She paused. "What'd he talk about?"

"He asked, could I take eleven inches," I said.

"Wow!"

"What am I, a mare?"

"Men," she said.

"It's because of them we have such hard lives," I said. "I ought to know. Two husbands, one bozo twice. And he just landed in the Indiana Pen, so his alimony's all dried up. I've got $3.76 to feed three little girls and me."

"What'll you do?"

"For starters, call the commune where Jenny's sorry father lives, and see if I can't pry something out of him. Errol Shiflet may not give a damn about me or Lonzo's two girls, but he wouldn't starve his own."

"Don't be too sure," Miss Willett said. "If a man wants revenge, there isn't anything he won't stoop to. But you need the phone."

"Damned if I want to look at Errol and his sea of tropical fish," I said.

"I can give you till three p.m. tomorrow. That's it, or I'll lose this job."

"Honey, us women have to stick together," I said.

"Whoops, supervisor's wading back from his fifteenth coffee break. Need more help, call me."

"Becky, you're a lifesaver."

"This job makes me feel like a criminal," she said. Then hung up.

Why I didn't order her to shut off my phone is beyond me. Because I had gotten a phone call the night before, though not a dirty one, like I told Becky Willett to get her sympathy.

It had come around ten, when Marlene at last flounced to bed after heating the phone lines with her fifty boy friends. I was already between the sheets studying for night school, reading a filthy novel set in Paris, France, by a dirty author who used his own name for the main character. He had the mind of a snake and a boaster's sense of shame, so I didn't need to dig for the hot parts. I was thinking how the beard would prickle over this one, when the phone started ringing like hell.

"Darling, that you?" A strong voice, like someone trained to berate crowds.

"Sure," I said.

"Look, I'm sorry I got so violent. Would you forgive me? Let me come back home?" He got that out in one breath, like someone reading.

"I'll have to give you directions," I said.

His breathing shifted gears. "It took guts to call," he said. "Don't mock me."

I thought how Daddy, fishing the stone quarry, gave his pole a feeble tug, not sure his hook had pricked the fish. "If you men learned how to hold your temper," I said, "maybe you wouldn't always have your tail between your legs."

"Maria?" he asked.

"Don't bet on it."

"Jesus," he sighed. "If one woman isn't fooling you, another jumps right in. Lucky, lucky, lucky. I'm pouring this boy another shot of wine."

"Probably what got you in trouble with what's-her-name. I've had two drinking men for husbands, so I know how snake oil changes a person's mood."

"Don't need a jealous husband after me," he said. "Not with my luck."

It felt like time to put up my guard. I knew what could come from strange men on the phone. Some screwball wrong-numbered one of Joy Silverspring's divorced friends while she was looped, came over, laid her smack dab on her own living room sofa, and staggered out without tipping his hat. "Listen," I said, "it's time you hung up."

"I want to ah talk," he said.

"Talk to Maria."

"She'd just refuse to forgive my sins. Who needs it?"

"For all I know, mister, you're Jack the Ripper."

"That scourge of God is roasting in hell. Why so suspicious of your fellow man?"

"You must be awful young," I said.

"Maybe a woman with your experience could teach me a few tricks," he chuckled.

"You have a wicked laugh."

"Like Hitler, the Anti-Christ." He switched into an Englishman's voice easy as an actor. "Adolf Hitler is a wicked, wicked man."

"There's wickedness everywhere. A mother of daughters has to be on her toes."

"Mother? Of daughters? How old are they?"

"None of your business," I said. "That'd be letting on how old I am."

"So you're a mother. No doubt you're aging like the finest wine, Mother." Then he took off down another path. "Biggest problem we have in this country is sex. It's our false god. You can't buy a magazine or ride a bus these days without having your face rubbed in sex. Lord, I'm lonely."

"You sound smart," I said. "Maybe you're too shy. Women need a little prodding to come round."

"Bless you, child, you have a good heart. What I need is a woman like you to give me back confidence."

"Hold that tiger, Jasper," I said. "You're a complete stranger. I don't mean to hurt your feelings, but no thanks."

"But you're tempted, Mother. Confess you're tempted."

I laughed. "Will you feel better if I say yes?"

"If it's true," he said.

"Well, yes."

"That's what I wanted to hear," he said.

"It's a good thing you don't know who I am, where I live, or my phone number," I told him. "You might come over."

The young man chuckled that devilish little chuckle. "Keep your doors locked."

"They are. Good and tight."

"Tomorrow night, then."

"Fresh thing. Hang up." I waited.

Then for no reason, he asked, "Didn't you worship James Dean when you were young?"

"We're both Hoosiers," I said, "me and James Dean."

"But I love him. Don't you love him?"

"James Dean is a corpse," I said. "Killed in a car wreck."

"Yes. By someone named Donald Turnipseed," said the man. "How would you like being done in by a seed?"

"You're a weirdo," I said, feeling eerie and slightly terrified. "You're plain out of your mind."

"I look just like James Dean," he persisted. "Won't you let me do till he's resurrected? Can't I be your rebel without a cause? Remember *East of Eden*? When he took his brother Aaron to the whorehouse to meet their long lost mother who was the madam?" And suddenly he almost busted my eardrum screaming, "Aaaaaaa-ron!"

Banging down the receiver, I reached into my nightstand drawer and rummaged among the crap till I felt Joe Palooka's limestone middle finger, which years ago, when we were going steady, Lonzo chipped off the statue high on a cliff outside Bedford, Indiana, and gave me, tied with a red bow. "To keep off the heebee jeebees," Lonzo Biggs had joked. I'm not superstitious, but I warmed that heavy rock between my palms, for luck or healing, I don't know. You sure can act dumb when you want to.

CHAPTER 5

After Becky Willett called from the phone company, I pulled on a tight blue sweater, and a plaid skirt that showed half my thighs. Thank God I hadn't yet gone to flab. Having babies scarcely puckered my belly, and veins didn't noticeably scrawl my legs, though I was bound some day to disintegrate like that rip Ethel.

The kids had left me one slice of bread, and an egg. In the sink lay the squeezed half lemon, which Bess probably sucked. Bess has unnatural tastes for a child and once ate a jar of sliced dills, gouging them in peanut butter like she was pregnant. Her stomach never gets queasy. Like me, she can digest brimstone.

I fried the egg in some lard, and also slathered lard on the bread, imitating Ethel's habit. Then I ate the puckered apple and washed down breakfast with a glass of water.

After brushing my teeth and touching red on my lips, I went out. Usually my street smells nasty, though we live two miles from Elm City's center and three from any factories pumping smoke into the sky and crud into Long Island Sound. But that morning the air was so fresh I might have been back home in Indiana with my daddy, swimming myself clean in quarry water or romping where the fall wheat ripened. This thought really bucked me up as I walked under tall oaks and maples toward Gorgeous George's, to hustle food on credit.

George and wife ran a cubbyhole market, Champion's, two blocks from my house. The overhead bell tinkled when I walked in, the only customer there. Holding a huge knife all glossy with blood, George hulked big and handsome behind the glassed-in meat at the store's rear.

"Mrs. Shiflet-Biggs!" he boomed, like I was some rich Englishwoman. Gorgeous had been my grocer ever since Errol and I got married. He was my grocer when I kicked Errol and his man-eating fish out, when I remarried Lonzo, then dumped him, too.

"Hello, George, how's tricks?"

"What tricks have you in mind?"

His wife, a sweet motherly butterball who, when George wasn't looking, slipped free apples, suckers and bologna slices into my grocery sack, smiled around one side of a cash register so ancient the wood had petrified. She was too short to see over the top, though her husband jutted six feet five inches, with jumbo gut under his clean white apron. "How are your little sweethearts, Mrs. Biggs?" she asked.

"There was enough in the icebox to give them breakfast this morning," I said. "But Lord knows where I'll find them supper."

"Supper?" hollered Gorgeous George, neatly slicing a kidney. Behind him, the wood door to the meat locker stood firmly shut. "What about breakfast tomorrow, and breakfast again?"

"It's why I'm here, George, as you well know. We've got to work a deal, or my three girls will starve."

"Oh, no, Mrs. Biggs!" cried Mrs. Champion. "Mr. Champion and I won't allow that."

But George, who always acted as if his wife wasn't in the same solar system with him, boomed out, "That responsibility is yours alone, Mrs. Shiflet-Biggs. After all, I'm not your father, am I? The good Lord has charged myself and Mrs. Champion with feeding our own twelve children, bred with the sweat of honest toil." He rammed that big knife splat into the small kidney.

Mrs. Champion shuddered. "Oh."

I walked to the meat counter and pressed my front against the glass. "George, I've been shopping here thirteen years."

"My unlucky number," said George.

"Hard luck sure has been hitting me lately."

George smiled, showing off two rows of straight, clean teeth. "What hard luck?"

I appealed to Mrs. Champion. "Remember Marlene's female trouble, that ran our doctor bill up so high?"

"Poor little thing," Mrs. Champion said.

"And what else, Mrs. Shiflet-Biggs?" George's head stuck close to his shoulders, the neck thick like a bull's.

"The kicker is, Lonzo stopped paying alimony."

"Typical low-class behavior, no offense. I see only one way out, which you should have thought of years ago."

"What, George?"

"You must get a job, dear lady. It is time to meet the real world."

"What *have* I been facing all these years, tell me that!" I wailed.

"A free ride," George told me, "on the wallets of men. Look at Mrs. Champion"—he stared at the meat—"mother of twelve, yet every spare minute of her time is spent here toiling to support her family." The Champions lived in four small rooms above the market.

"Oh dear sweet Lord," I murmured.

"A job," he said quietly, eyeing me like I was a side of USDA prime.

"What kind, George?"

"There are a million jobs, Mrs. Shiflet-Biggs." He glanced at the meat locker. "Regular jobs. Odd jobs. Like helping a businessman straighten up his stock. Perhaps, with children still in school, what you want is an odd job."

"How odd?"

"One which suits your own peculiar talent." His big hands stroked his big belly.

My insides itched, because I knew Mrs. Champion was looking hard at me from behind, and suddenly I remembered the dream Joy Silverspring told me about. Joy dreamed hairless white dogs were lying in George's meat trays, like dachshunds with their feet chopped off, eyes shut tight, and George would hold up one after another for her to choose. But Joy said, "Oh, no, that one's way too big for my family. Oh, no, I don't think we could handle that one either, it's so huge!" This happened during one of those times Joy's husband Michael was trying like crazy to get her pregnant, as usual without the slightest bit of luck. "Now, why do you suppose I'd dream that, Amelia?" she asked, these blank innocent holes in her eyeballs like cat eyes, and she graduated college, too. It had almost killed me, holding the laughter in. "I wouldn't eat a dog to save my soul!" Joy Silverspring had cried.

Now I backed away from George. "Your sweet wife," I said. "Twelve babies knocked out of her in twelve years, you horny toad. It's a good thing she's so full of love."

"Bless you," Mrs. Champion whispered.

"And me with nothing in the icebox but a dish covered over with wax paper, that I don't even dare open up to throw away, what's inside is so rotten and awful by now."

"Let me give you a little something," Mrs. Champion said, rapidly throwing open the dairy case and reaching for some Vermont cheese.

"Not so fast, Mrs. Champion!" George froze her on tiptoes.

"Not so fast yourself, you old degenerate," I said and stamped through the door. A young priest, on furlough maybe from the monastery, had to skip out of my path. "Excuse me, Father," I said.

Walking home, I noticed how the area was falling apart. This used to be one of Elm City's poshest neighborhoods. Now the big fine homes were so far gone no medicine could perk them up. Windows of a fire-gutted pair gaped blindly—bats that whirled around the lampposts at night now slept here. Some houses were three times bigger than mine, mansions with enough rooms to hold three whole Champion litters in comfort. Once there were velvet curtains, servants, dollars in grand piles, gobs of food, ladies who never had "job" mentioned in their hearing. Now the mansions are antheaps, chopped into welfare cells. Having a whole house, I guess I'm lucky, though the neighborhood hadn't decayed so thirteen years before when Errol Shiflet moved us and the tropical sea in. Wood and brick and stone, man-made things crumbling into heaps of rubble, all the elms dead of blight and the big trees that were left sickening toward bare, dead winter.

It made me recall that statue of Joe Palooka I mentioned earlier. When I was a girl, some fools in Bedford, twenty miles south of Goldengrove, Indiana, where I was born and brought up, squandered tax money to have stonecutters hack out a twelve-ton cartoon, because they said Joe Palooka stood for everything that America loved and admired, bull muscle and stupidity, I suppose, as if you need something to look up to, even if it's a funnybook, Batman or Daddy Warbucks. Anyway, Joe stood like St. Peter on a cliff overlooking Route 37, and baited more than one poor family to its doom, cracked up on that twisty road as they yelled, "There's Joe Palooka!" But Ham Fisher, who drew the strip, got haled before Coonskin Kefauver for drawing an eight-page Bible that showed Li'l Abner ramming his pole into Daisy Mae—Al Capp, no less, hooked Fisher with the rap—so Ham blew his own brains out. Soon boys scaled the face of that big rock to knock pieces off their example, because it's fun to tear things apart. They reduced Joe to a torn-down mess, like Superman blasted with Kryptonite, a hunk of the planet he'd been born on.

Lonzo gave me the limestone middle finger three days after I learned my daddy had died, when I felt that nothing could ever heal my wound.

CHAPTER 6

Mounting the porch, where our five green plastic trash barrels sat, I found I'd forgotten to lock the front door. The Cat Burglar, who had recently started robbing stores and houses and leaving silly poems behind, could have swiped everything of value, mainly the Zenith charged from Macy's. Or some rapist could be standing in a closet cool as a snake, to do his dirty work. I stole inside fast. But my Zenith sat in the dining room, safe and sound, and no rapist jumped me. Alone without a man, I needed a big watchdog, except that high-strung purebreds, like Dobermans, gave me the willies. With this bland, empty look in their eyes, Dobermans sometimes eat babies out of their cradles. Errol once said his fish made vicious watchdogs. "By Jesus," he would rave, "if some burglar breaks in, I'll feed his shit and bones to my lovely Red Devil!" Looking around my shabby living room, I saw empty space where those huge tanks once bubbled and Errol's gorgeous, empty-eyed monsters hung in midair.

It was time to get in touch with the poor S.O.B. Becky Willett let me keep my phone so I wouldn't have to face Errol, but old Ethel, tough saleswoman, counseled frontal attack in important matters, which meant throwing your whole body into battle. The apple didn't fall that far from the tree. So I went back out. My Chevy took its time starting, and a gray thunderhead puffed up behind.

32

Errol Shiflet, Ph.D., lived on the other side of Elm City, in a share-and-share-alike commune, with a few university students whom he'd taught. Back when universities were blowing like swamp gas, Errol became the most popular teacher at Elm City U, a hero and student idol. For one thing, he decided that papers, tests, and grades weren't fair, maybe because some people were more stupid than others —so the first day he had his classes vote a final grade for everybody. They voted for A, which their messiah gave them. When six hundred students enrolled in his lit discussion course, the university grade-point average popped its cork. He trained his creative writing class to be burglars, or guerrillas, because living was better than writing, and one midnight he and a dozen students, all juiced up for revolution, overthrew the university radio station halfway through a Beatles record. Some poor disc jockey must have crapped his jeans. It was during that period that I kicked Errol out.

Errol also debated the university president and members of the board of trustees. He sat barefoot before a thousand people and called those dignified, fatherly men "shriveled, impotent pinheads," and "invidious fuckbrains." "I'm the most powerful man on campus, Amelia," Errol once boasted when he came to visit Jenny. "If those farts try to fire me, I'll blow this whole goddamn town sky-high!"

But that was a few years before. And now Errol was supposedly on leave from the university, writing a book to prove that all great novels made you want to murder somebody. I also heard rumors that people didn't exactly worship him anymore.

The commune was a huge Victorian house built of fieldstone, with two turrets like a castle, and a green slate roof. A porch hooded three whole sides. Across the road lay a filthy beach, and Long Island Sound, cool and still. A sign jammed into the sand said, "Polluted, No Swimming." All in all, this was a ritzy settlement, especially summers when the rich who owned these houses crawled up from New York City. By September, though, the plutocrats had left. Most of the houses stood empty and ripe for thieves and vandals, which I suppose is why this owner might have tolerated a commune.

Four sleek sports cars were parked at the curb, a Jaguar, a Mercedes, and the other two, emerald and ruby, so fancy I didn't know their make. Trapped among them sat Errol's bunged-up black Morris. A van, "Frank's Frozen Meat" on its side, stood in the yard, and nearby two boys and two girls played volleyball. A man in blue work clothes lugged a metal basket of white-wrapped parcels out of the van's rear onto the porch, where several baskets were already piled by the side door.

One of the boys yelled, "Hey, Chick, how's it going?" He caught the volleyball, tucked it under one arm, and with his free hand flicked long blond hair out of his eyes.

I got out of my car. "Where's Errol Shiflet?" I called.

"How come a stacked chick like you wants old Errol?" the boy yelled back.

"Shut up, Bill," said the other boy.

I stepped around hunks of dog crap in the scraggly grass.

"Errol's inside, lady," said a skinny girl in blue jeans and a T-shirt. No bra held her little tits in line.

"Old Errol's recuperating from hot clap!" yelled Bill, butting the ball over the fishnet with his thick skull.

The meat man set down another basket, shook his head, then shuffled back to the van. The other girl, a redhead, said, "Bill's got the mental power of two sticks clicking together."

"Dope," said Bill.

"Clickety-click," said the redhead.

I walked to the side door and knocked against a glass panel. Icy air flowed from the several-hundred-pound stack of frozen meat beside me.

"Door's unlocked," called the nicer boy.

A huge golden retriever attacked me in the kitchen. His forelegs gripped my rib cage. A tongue slopped my face, and the dog humped me rambunctiously against the wall. "Hold on there, Rover!" I yelled, shoving him away. Rover licked my shoes, whimpered, and banged his giant gold feather of a tail against a table leg. I breathed a thick aroma of dog, stewed in with a pigsty of other smells, including fish. All at once, Errol Shiflet, red-eyed, stood in the kitchen doorway like a giant spider.

"By sweet Jesus, I saw it," he cried. "Working your way up to donkeys. Here, Zeus," he told Rover. "Go upstairs and fuck the cat." The dog loped away, into uncut gloom.

"Errol, what would happen to the natural order if you changed the slush filter in your mouth?"

But he had changed. The last time I delivered Jenny here, because Errol's car broke down, he had been strong and powerful. Packs of muscle had tightened through his shirt whenever he thought something so filthy that merely spitting it out would bring the sky thundering down around his hairy ears. All the commune girls had climbed over him like he was solid Spanish fly. So what if their little hotpants were full of gunk? Errol was king of the hive, licking the honey up. Why I'd lost my temper that time is beyond me. But I'd told him if he wanted to see Jenny anymore, send one of the filthy A-rabs he lived with to pick her up at home, because I never wanted to see his thick nose again.

Now Errol was a pitiful sight, wearing baggy, frayed blue jeans, down-at-the-heels workboots, and a green shirt he wore years back when we were still married. "You must have lost fifty pounds," I said. "Don't these little trollops know how to cook?"

"I'm on a pussy-eating diet," said Errol with an unhealthy grin.

"And I may throw up."

"Why? You've screwed everything in trousers. Goddamn hillbilly hypocrite." But he acted like he was only going through the motions of being nasty, for old times' sake. "Ah shit!" Errol snorted. "Twilight of the gods. I'm fucking sick, and that's a goddamn fact."

Outside, the meat truck rumbled to a start and drove away.

"Let's go sit somewhere," I said.

"Naw, let's lie down and screw," Errol said, without

much pep. "Must be why you came, the way you're dressed."

"Maybe if you didn't have such a dirt-track mind," I said, "the two of us would have been better at it together."

Errol scratched the scar on his throat and growled, "A moral lecture from the Whore of Babylon?"

He shuffled into another room. I followed. "How's your fish, Errol?"

"Sick, too." Errol made for a fat, worn, brown-velvet couch that came from King Tut's tomb. When we sat, dust billowed up.

"No medicine worked worth shit on my Red Devil," he said, "so I fed her out of the other tanks. For a while she did all right on ten-dollar tropical fish. Finally I ran out of everything except the two piranha, so I fed her those, one at a time. She's all I have left." Errol bought his Red Devil the last year we were married and fed the filthy thing fifty live goldfish a week. When you walked in, the Red Devil bopped its tank trying to break out and eat you. "Another child for Moloch," Errol would say, pitching a fish into the cannibal's tank. Moloch's jaws clacked like an ax hitting the block.

"Is it dead?" I asked now.

"Nah. We sleep upstairs together. If I pulled her teeth, she'd give fantastic blow jobs."

Bill pranced in dribbling a volleyball against the dark floor. "If it isn't Errol," he said, "crawled out from under his rock."

"Hi, Bill," Errol muttered, downcast and embarrassed.

"Well, hi yourself." Bill dribbled the ball at Errol's toes. "How's the Hong Kong clap?"

"Cut it out," Errol said. The Errol I married would have decked the little bastard, who couldn't have been twenty yet.

"Hey, Errol, I didn't know you could still get stuff like this."

"Commune's population turns over all the time," Errol told me, trying to get Bill off his back.

"Old Errol's gonna be freeloading here till 2001, right, Errol?" And the stripling blew out.

"How come you let him talk that way?" I asked.

"Dunno."

"One of those fancy cars his?"

"The Ferrari. Twenty grand worth of dead steel." Then Errol clammed up completely, which was unlike Errol. Even while daydreaming, he used to cut loose a "Shit!" or two just to knock holes in the air.

Finally I said, "Listen, Errol, I want to apologize for Marlene's smartass remark to your mother."

"What I want to know," he said, "is why didn't she have a go at my snakebrained old man, that shriveled, impotent pinhead, that—" He gagged, trying to think up a name horrible enough. "I'd feed that fucker's balls to my Red Devil one at a time. And you know the old bastard's retired now and flying in any day to spy on me?"

Back when I was five months gone with Jenny, Errol drove me and Marlene, nearly four, to Columbus, Ohio, his home town, to meet his parents for the first time. Errol's old man, an M.D., lived in Upper Arlington, the town's swankest section, but talk about low class! When Errol was a child, the old bastard used to hold him upside down over the john and threaten to flush him if he misbehaved. Errol believed it. What do kids know, except what their parents teach them? Anytime he heard Errol cuss, the old man fed him soap. Some parents wash their kids' mouths out, but Errol's pop, the Doctor of Medicine, would make him chew up the whole bar. When Errol was twelve, the fool crammed a bar down Errol's throat, where it jammed, and Errol began choking to death in the bathroom. So Dr. Shiflet knocked the blue-blade loose from his Gillette and performed emergency surgery on his son and heir, slashed Errol's windpipe so he could breathe, then lied to the hospital, "I simply cannot imagine how my son came to be eating that Ivory soap." Some of us have a worse time than others, and though Errol is surely one torn-down fool, he can't change his breeding, any more than Lonzo can change his, or I can change mine, or that Red Devil can change hers.

So I was prepared for quite a bit, but Errol had neglected

mentioning the snakes, knowing I wouldn't have made the trip then. And he was aching to kill his old man with jealousy, he said, when the S.O.B. saw his own son, as Errol put it on our way there, "driving balls-deep into Mother Earth." While courting me, Errol had kept his tongue on a leash, but since we married he kept getting more foul-mouthed each day.

Dr. Shiflet, who considered himself an all-around man of culture, lover of art and fine wine, was also a snake collector, practice limited to rattlers, water moccasins, copperheads, and boa constrictors, swarming with lice. He boarded a couple-hundred live, red-eyed white mice for lizard food. Thousands extra slept in the deepfreeze. In an emergency, he'd thaw a few on the range.

We hit Columbus at feeding time, so before dinner Dr. Shiflet invited us to watch his reptiles chow down. It was interesting, in a shameful way. Take the copperhead. The mouse sniffed madly around the cage, the snake still as ice. Suddenly I heard "Thump!" though I saw nothing move, and the mouse pricked up, like a man standing before a huge crowd with his fly unzipped, wondering why everyone's buzzing. Starting at its tail, the mouse stiffened, till only his red eyes could move. Then the snake unhinged its jaw. Slowly it sucked the mouse in head first. Errol loved the show. "Nature is inspiring in her ugly ways!" he told the old man. Then he said something that even shocked me. "Where are this luscious piece and I sleeping, Dad? My boyhood room, that graveyard of dead sperm?" I already knew Errol had a raunchy mind, but I didn't learn how deep the dirt really went till I saw him face to face with his father. Later, when the revolution made Errol completely over into Mr. Hyde, and he started sleeping with anything in hotpants, I finally had to divorce him.

Snakes lined the walls of Errol's old room in cages, and that was in fact where we bedded down, Marlene in a crib beside us, Jenny in my belly. "I won't be able to sleep a wink," I said. But Errol insisted. It appealed to his perverted taste, and Dr. Shiflet promised nothing could get out.

After Errol had done things I won't describe, I lay stiff with fear as something rustled across the floor. I yelled. Errol flicked on his light. About the bed writhed a clot of night-crawlers, like a hard rain had washed them up. Hearing me screech, Dr. Shiflet made a night call, setting a goblet of purple wine on Errol's dresser, and diving for his pets.

"Baby copperheads," he gasped, as they snapped his palms, "don't have the sting of a honeybee."

But I reared up on the mattress, sheet wrapping my naked body, and gave the bald old wino what for. Errol laughed and whispered, "Sic him!" and Errol's mom appeared smiling at the bedroom door, rooting silently for the kill, while in hot fury I told Dr. Shiflet he was murdering his unborn grandchild like he almost murdered his son. Later, as I threw our clothes together for a quick getaway, Errol crooned, "By sweet Jesus, Amelia, you ripped those wrinkled balls from his body. You ate him alive."

Now I said, "Easy, Errol," because he still gagged with fury. "That old codger's damaged you enough."

The redheaded girl, followed by the nicer boy, wandered into the room. Errol scrunched his knees against his chin. "Hello, Donna," he said.

"Uh, hi." She looked at Errol like he was a toadstool.

"I'd like you to meet Amelia, Donna. You, too, Jimmy."

"Hi," Jimmy said. "Sorry about Bill."

"I know the type," I said. "All shirt and no pants."

"Pretty good," murmured the redhead, languid and lazy. "I'll have to use that one myself."

"Donna, this beautiful woman is my former wife," said Errol, as if anybody had asked.

"Impressed. Terribly." The redhead shrugged. "Jimmy, let's climb out of these sweaty clothes."

"Hey!" Jimmy followed her out.

"Did you hear that?" Errol frothed. "Right in front of me? Asking Jimmy up to ball."

"So what, Errol?"

Errol groaned, "God, that woman's tearing me apart and she doesn't care."

"She couldn't be nineteen yet."

"Jesus, she's beautiful and brilliant and balling a kid who needs his nose wiped."

"Errol, is it true you caught clap?"

"Yes."

"From her?"

"She won't look at me. I don't know whose branding iron it was."

"I'm not surprised," I said. "These young harlots never heard about washing."

"Six months ago I was up in my bed having a sex dream, and suddenly I'm awake with this real live girl sitting on my prick. Total stranger. When I shoot off, she runs naked and laughing from the room. I'm so shocked I don't even follow. Pretty soon a car peals out. A week later, I'm oozing with clap. It's that fuckhead Bill, I'm sure. My ashes hadn't been hauled for a month, and he knew it. So he hustled some diseased girl friend out here to give me this little present."

"Can't they cure it?" I felt all flustered, as if the same thing had once happened to me on some black, unremembered night, and branded its mark in my brain.

"I'm so allergic to penicillin and the mycins, one shot'll stop my heart. Anyway, it's some oriental bug in chain mail that battens on all antibiotics. So I'm completely boxed in. I should execute Bill for attempted murder. Inhuman chaos is eating me alive. Come on up. I'll show you my room, where it happened."

I followed Errol up a winding staircase like a lighthouse. From wood walls pictures hung crumbling in their frames, girls with wide, ground-length skirts, pinched lips, cowsize eyeballs, all so neatly in place it didn't belong to my earth. "This old joint is a period piece," I said.

"Yah," filthy-minded Errol laughed, "messy and slick. Man needs nonskid rubbers to tool down that blood-drenched highway."

We reached a dismal long hall. Behind a shut door, I heard people screwing. The next door stood open, and I saw a wad of greenbacks on the mattress.

"Bait," Errol said. "Bill's room. The shit wants me to steal his money. He is definitely what the mackerel-snappers would call an occasion of sin." Suddenly he nailed my eyes with his. "Woman, if you're hustling me for money, you are out of luck."

"Oh, Errol, what makes you think such a thing?"

"Those bastard trustees burned my contract. Drew my final check two months ago. Ah, here's the shithole that holds my bod."

It stank of sweat, stale beer breath, and dog. Zeus slept on Errol's torn-up bed, and curled before his snout lay a Siamese cat. Socks, pants, shirts, paper, whiskey bottles, crushed Dixie cups and mungballs sowed a room that measured ten by ten. A gray window glared east over Long Island Sound, across which I made out the faint sawteeth of buildings.

In the room's middle stood a twenty-gallon tankful of dun water. With delicate fins like wings, a two-pound, frantic, reddish-black slab of man-eating fish bopped the glass, crazy for a bite of warm meat.

"Long time no see, Moloch," I said. "Looks like we're being taken care of the same way."

"Tried mating her with an eighty-five-buck fucker six months ago," Errol said. "Guess he wasn't well hung enough, because she ate him up."

"You only give me sixty-five a month for Jenny."

"Gave," said Errol. "Find a job, or Jenny'll have to go on that diet for good."

"Errol, what is the matter with you?" I yelled. The dog groaned, the cat flicked its tail, the Red Devil churned the filthy water white, its jaws snapping through the foam. "Look what's happening to your life! You insult those old trustees and lose your job, then fall in love with a baby. I'd rip these walls down to feed my kids!"

Flopping beside the dog and cat, Errol looked so down I almost felt sorry for him. "Wasn't I an interesting man once?" he asked. "Even attractive?"

"Yes, honey, it's hard to believe. And you still would be, if you weren't such a roaring dumbass."

In bounced Bill wearing only his birthday suit. "Hey there, dollface," he leered, pointing down at his bare self. "Know what that is?"

I'd had it completely with this bozo. "Sure," I said. "A small peter."

"Gee whillikers." Bill faded into the hall. In a few moments, a car started outside and drove away.

Errol and I faced each other in silence. Finally he said, "You wonderful balleater!" It shocked me to see tears pouring from his bloodshot, clapridden eyes, down his wasted cheeks. The Red Devil pounded like a sledgehammer at the glass, trying to gobble Errol. Suddenly the whole room swam, as if my head and body floated apart.

"It's all too goddamn much!" I shouted.

Then in another room I bent over a mattress, Bill's bait in both my hands. A dog woofed. Someone yelled. I sailed downstairs and heard crashing all round. Pictures tumbled off the walls. My feet munched glass and dusty paper.

Free of the house I felt an iciness freezing my breasts. The meat truck had gone, and one of the fancy sports jobs had flown the curb. The net stretched empty between its posts. Way out on the filthy Sound a sail moved slowly like a sharkfin, and a one-engine airplane droned free in the bright-blue air, and I thought again of the pure limestone quarries of home where I'd felt so clean of guilt. A rock tongue stuck into the water. Gulls whirled over it, dropping clams to bust the shells.

My car seat felt firm like Daddy's lap. On the rotten upholstery where I must just have pitched them, I saw white packages, steaming cold, that I'd stolen without even knowing what I was about, and clumps of Bill's dollars like seaweed.

My Chevy crumpled the sports job in front. I backed, then smashed it again, raked another's side, and tore viciously into the front car. "Wheeeee!" I cried, making my getaway slick as a greased mole.

CHAPTER 7

A half hour later, hugging the icy packets, I floated on my new high spirits through the dingy mess of my living room and dining room into the kitchen, where I found Joy Silverspring lounging at my table, chain-smoking Eves, and grinding her fags out on my breakfast dishes. Sun poured in from the west. I almost saw angels and cupids breast-stroking through the thick, boiling clouds of tobacco smoke.

"Amelia!" she cried. "I have the most incredibly wonderful news." My old friend one street over, Joy was the happiest person I had ever met in my life.

"Hey there! That's wonderful news, all right!" I could hardly wait to count my treasure. As soon as the commune was out of sight, I had straightened the loot pile and stuffed it down my panties.

"But you don't know what it is," Joy Silverspring said.

"I know I don't. But it's wonderful anyway!" I stowed the meat in my icebox freezer, then plopped down across from Joy. Paper crunched between my thighs.

"Michael and I are getting a baby boy."

"But I thought your husband shot blanks," I said.

"Will you quit acting crazy?" Joy squeezed her hands together. "We're adopting a child, three months old."

"Whose poor little girl," I wondered out loud, "got broken into this time?"

"Come on, Amelia. It's the happiest day of my life."

"What color is the baby?" I remembered what Joy had told me a few months back.

"Well, that's a problem," Joy said. "We specified some race nobody else would adopt. But the only thing they had on hand was white, and that's better than nothing at all."

"But is it at least deformed?" I asked. Joy sometimes acted like she wanted, more than anything else in the world, to punish herself for a crime she couldn't name, because she had completely forgotten what it was.

"That's another problem," Joy said. "We told them we wanted some poor defective baby, a clubfoot or a cleft palate, because nobody else would. But this one is perfect, I'm ashamed to say." She actually looked ashamed, which was unlike Joy. I recalled five years earlier, when Joy Silverspring visited me in the hospital after I'd had Bess. There I lay nursing the loveliest little baby, and Joy looked at Bess, then acted embarrassed and didn't speak at all till she was leaving, when she said, "It has hairy ears."

But Joy wasn't such a bad old egg, considering that husband of hers, who I hadn't seen, mercifully, for over a month. Joy first noticed the poor mutant when they were students at some small Baptist college in Indiana—like me, Joy is a Hoosier. In one class sat the mangiest, smelliest young man ever, and Joy, the arrow already in her heart, thought, "There's somebody who needs taking care of." Michael's mother died giving him birth. His father had been a ranting, drunken atheist who burned down the local Baptist church and got sent to the Indiana Pen, where he later died, but not before getting converted and confessing to the prison chaplain that at least once during a drunken fit the old degenerate had molested his own son. So I had to pity Michael a little at least. The experience had been so awful that Michael made himself forget. A shrinker, plus a letter from the chaplain, had done him the favor of reminding him. He confided in Joy, and Joy passed the information on to me.

Anyway, Joy ripped after Michael like a torn-down pig. They got married at nineteen and became the happiest pair in the world.

For instance, Michael's big wide body could be parked five rooms away from Joy, and he'd drop his pencil. "Joy-eeee!" he'd yell. "I dropped my pencil!" And Joy would come running, pick up the pencil lying right at Michael's big feet, and croon to her Mongolian in diapers, "Oh, here, sweetheart darling."

While Michael was still in grad school, before he got a job in Errol's department and became a poet, they announced that the best way to live was stay up all night and sleep all day. "There isn't any other possible method," Joy told me. "At night, there aren't distractions. You can get ten times as much done." But a few months later, they'd turned it all around, went to bed at 6 P.M. and got up at 6 A.M. "It's the only natural way to run your life," Joy insisted. "We're so rested, we can get ten times as much done as before." Then they fixed their sights on eating. Joy would bustle around for hours concocting huge French dinners. After a while even skinny Joy grew a deformed belly, like she was pregnant. "It's the only way to live," she told me. "Michael and I have never been happier in our lives." Her husband, like a circus freak, blimped up so gross and oily that if you touched a match to him he'd burn like napalm.

Suddenly they were only eating lettuce and brown rice, both wasted like Displaced Persons, and Joy told me, "How can you go on eating, Amelia? Food'll take twenty years off your life."

The year I first met the Silversprings, they were mad dogs on the subject of capital punishment. When the governor let a black rapist cool his lifetime away in the clink, rather than roast him, Joy and Michael shot off bloodthirsty letters to newspapers all over the state. "Where the governor went especially wrong," they wrote, "was in not demanding an even more extreme penalty, to match the crime. Why was the offender not publicly castrated, then dismembered by wild horses tied to each of the offender's limbs and made to run toward the four points of the compass? Joy and Michael Silverspring." Shoplifters should have their hands chopped off, they said, and live rats should be sewn inside traitors' bellies. When I argued that their ideas were completely disgusting, they said I was a greater criminal than an ordinary murderer. After a few years, though, they pulled the old switcheroo. On the Green a couple of summers before, I'd spotted Michael and Joy, a spaced-out stare in their eyes, parading with signs behind a dozen weirdos before the police station. The other signs had bones to pick about one poor kid pulling ten years for burning his draft card. But Michael's sign read, CRIME IS AN ACT OF GOD, and Joy's, ALL FREE PEOPLE ARE CRIMINALS.

Then came the cats. Joy hadn't understood how Errol could keep fish. "It's selfish," she said, "wasting money on lower creatures, when we ought to be looking after our fellow human beings." But they began feeding a stray female cat, which cut loose a litter of nine, half with some deformity Joy's vet called the "Ithaca mutation," which gave them opposing thumbs on their front paws. Joy decided it would be inhuman to give any away. "Who knows what might happen to the poor little things?" she asked. "Besides, we're all part of nature. We're animals, too, and nobody can be fully human without loving other animals." So in spite of the fact that Joy was a maniac for neatness, they bedded down with six huge geldings and four fat spays lolling all over their house and eating off Joy's dinner plates and shitting everywhere.

Now I said, "It's wonderful about your baby, Joy. But won't it get in the cats' way?"

"Oh, that isn't any problem," said Joy. "We shipped them all to the Humane Society."

"Lord, what did Michael say?"

"First he cried. Then he argued that we ought to keep at least one. But I told him, sparing that cat wasn't fair to the others. Once you've stepped across the line, you might as well go all the way."

"The whole hog," I said.

"Yes. If you commit a crime that throws you beyond the pale, you might as well keep going." Joy twisted her hands

46

together. "By the way, Michael has begun imitating Christ like a fool. He carries a Bible everywhere." She lit another fag from a butt and sucked mightily. Smoke shot from her nose like tusks. As usual, her clothes were crisp and neat, a starchy white blouse that choked her wrists and neck, and purple slacks whose crease could slice raw chicken. From time to time, Joy rubbed her arms and shoulders as if they hurt, making me wonder if Michael had beaten her up over the cats. But in spite of her skinniness, Joy was strong as Superwoman, and could have fought back like a tiger.

"Wish I could solve my problems like you," I said.

"It's a gift. There's nothing I can't put in its proper place. That's why I've never been unhappy in my whole life." She smiled. Through the smoke I saw her dark, deep pupils, like those of an ostrich I saw in the Bronx Zoo.

"Of course, it helps when you can't remember anything before you were twelve," I said. I knew only that Joy had an older sister, Bobbie Jo. The one time she mentioned her sister's name to me, because she said I kind of resembled Bobbie Jo, Joy had started trembling in an epileptic fit, as if one memory of her past would shrivel her like Kryptonite.

Now Joy said, "I was so happy, there's nothing to remember."

But I had seen Joy unhappy another time as well. Everything lay on her dresser in such religious neatness, she must have arranged her cold cream, perfume, brush, lipstick, mascara, deodorant, hand lotion, orange sticks, nail file, and breath spray with a T-square. It was one spot in the house where a curious cat could get murdered. Once, out of devilishness, I altered her orange sticks, rolled her lipstick over an inch, scooted her breath spray closer to the lozenges. I wouldn't have noticed any difference, but when Joy returned, you'd have thought the world had broken like Humpty Dumpty. "My God!" Joy yelled. "Who moved my lipstick?"

"A cat?"

"My breath spray!" She clouded a spot on the mirror.

"Jesus, those cats! I found one of those freaks holding a barrette in its front paws trying to stick the thing between its ears. I can't keep anything straight!"

"Why try?" I had asked. "Let it all go bust. It might be a mess of fun."

"I wasn't raaaaaised that way!" she wailed. "I didn't graduate from reform school. I haven't married three times and divorced the best husband in the world. I'd drown in the shambles. You let it all go bust if you want to. I'd wind up in a whorehouse." She'd paused. "But Jesus, I've got to do *something!*"

So she could repeat the private ceremony of T-squaring her gunk, she sent me home feeling like I'd glimpsed the real Joy.

Now she said, "You walked in like you're all sore, Amelia. Did somebody score, ha ha?"

"Went to see Errol for the first time in a year."

Joy's eyes shrank to penlight beams, and she hunched her back. "Did Errol—?"

"That poor loony'd need a grappling hook to catch me," I said. "No."

"Errol's not half as crazy as some people."

"He needs a keeper," I said. "He's all grimy, living with a bunch of mangy, smelly kids. His room looks like the H-bomb hit. He makes more noise than a pair of hung-up dogs, and he's sick with—something the doctors can't cure." For old times' sake, I barely controlled my mouth and kept Errol's clap to myself.

"I'm going to have my hands full with the new baby, maybe," Joy threw in from left field, and her eyes went blind again.

"You sure are. Wonder how Michael's going to feel with half his usual care and feeding."

"Oh, Michael doesn't need looking after," Joy said. "He bookworms at the library till twelve midnight. All day his nose is buried in the Bible he hauls everywhere like a second peter. A while back, he drove down to Rye, New York, and got converted to some wacky brand of Jesus by some creep who carried the gospel by motorcycle from Ohio. Now he's so holy he completely stopped banging me."

"Sounds like a candidate for the monastery," I said.

"That motel for horny monks," Joy said. "Oh, come, all ye faithful, ha ha."

Surely nobody would want Joy but Michael, and vice versa. What a shame if anything blew such a matched pair apart. "Nothing like a baby for playing Cupid," I said. "Really I'm so glad for you, honey." Though I was worried, for instance, that she and Michael might decide the only possible way to raise their baby was in a cage, feeding it organic cat food.

"Cupid? I'll take the one who socked it to Psyche," Joy said. "Well, I have to scoot and start plotting"—her pupils gaped—"a room for Baby."

I led her to the door.

"Sure something isn't wrong, Amelia? You walk like somebody lobbed a cob up your tail."

"You look sore yourself," I said. "What've you been into?"

"Another thing," she went on, "this neighborhood isn't what it was twelve years ago. Better be more careful about locking your doors, the Cat Burglar might clean you out. I turned the knob and walked right in . . . Wow! Who bashed your car?"

Ragged streaks, emerald and ruby, slashed the Chevy's white flank. "Perks the old junker up, doesn't it?" I said. "Must've been sideswiped when I was in with Errol."

"Not unless you parked on the wrong side of the street."

"That's a one-way out there."

"No, it is not," Joy Silverspring said.

"Poor old Errol. Somebody ought to send him a trained nurse."

"You could use one yourself," Joy said. "Your elbows are flying."

"What?"

"Flapping like the wings of a blind bird." Smoke blasted from Joy's snoot. "And since you clearly don't waste time cleaning house, why not get a job?"

All of a sudden, Joy seemed angry, and in spite of the dough in my drawers, I felt riled up, too.

"Get one yourself," I shot back. "I'm mighty tired of everybody telling me to get a job. What can a woman find these days?"

"A woman like you," purred Joy, "is clearly sitting on a fortune."

Which shocked me. Till I saw it was a blind shot, that Joy was jealous of my looks and all she meant was, Amelia Biggs is pretty enough to hustle her living as a common whore. Still, there was no percentage in fighting now. "I don't know what's got into you, Joy," I said. "But this isn't any time for us to claw each other, with good news about your baby."

At once Joy smiled like somebody had flipped a switch on her backbone. "Can't imagine what started us off," she said, giving me a big hug, cigarette packs and matchbooks clutched in both paws.

I hugged her, too. "Us women've got to look out for one another."

"That's the Lord God's truth." Joy kissed me wetly on the neck, which she'd done before and which always made me wonder. I'd seen enough fruitcake for a lifetime back in reform school. But Joy only bounced happily across the porch.

Wild and silly, I flapped my elbows back into the kitchen to cook a steak and count my change.

CHAPTER 8

The Lord God's Truth was, I felt so crazy for a bite I ripped like Errol's Red Devil into one of those white bundles. Three thick T-bones separated by green paper, a meat gold mine! Throwing a pair under the broiler in my old electric stove, I thought about those rich kids with their hot cars and careless lives, tons of steak to gobble while my girls and I might starve if I didn't scramble. I almost wanted to drive there tonight, after they'd screwed themselves to sleep, and silent as a cat plant bombs round their mansion and blow it back into fieldstone. Finally the meat thawed to body temperature. I wolfed it down, which put me in a better mood altogether.

As I got set to slide out my booty, the front door crashed open. At first I thought the cops were invading me, and quick as I could I emptied the bone crosses into my wastecan. But it was my girls, and one boy, stranger, holding Marlene's hand and shuffling on big duck feet. He wore a loose khaki shirt, open at the collar, and green pants with baggy knees.

"Something smells good," Marlene said.

"Sure does," agreed the boy, who looked in his early twenties.

Little Bess let go Jenny's hand, rushed over and gave me a powerful hug. "I love your big butt!"

"Watch that talk," I said.

Jenny leaned against the kitchen door. Her face looked like the A.C. had been shut off.

"Mamma, meet Jack," Marlene said. "He's in my high school."

"Jack Rader." He let go Marlene's hand and shook mine. The grip felt weird, like a spring clothespin twisted to meet crooked. "Awful pleased."

"He's back from the war, Mamma," Marlene said.

"Been in Nam four years, Mrs. Biggs. Three-year hitch plus a year out of a second. I was a high school junior when I signed. Thought I otta finish."

"A senior, Mamma." Marlene stood beside his chair. "Only one year ahead of your little girl."

"There ain't no jobs, Mrs. Biggs."

"And he's a hero," Jenny said slowly. "Won a Silver Star."

"Shee-ucks." Jack was tall, a thin-faced fellow whose wavy hair, I was glad to see, didn't hit his shoulders.

"All my life," Marlene took Jack Rader's hand, "I wanted to go out with a glorious hero."

"Marlene is a card, Mrs. Biggs. Smartest girl I seen."

"Jack doesn't have a thumb," Bess giggled. "Jack doesn't have a toe."

"Quiet down, Bess," I said. "Live with your folks?"

"Naw, they is dead," said Jack Rader. "Live alone in a partment near downtown. None of my family ever been here but me. We come from West Virginia."

"How can you afford not having any job?" The apartment worried me.

"Lord, Mamma. He isn't asking for my hand."

"Aw, Marlene. I git full disability, ma'am."

"Doesn't look all shot to pieces, does he, Mamma?" Marlene grinned.

"Ain't," Jack said. "Only thing, I can't throw the safety on a M-16. Now, my buddy who got his legs shot off gits less'n me, which don't make sense. But Sam sets the rules, not me."

Jack reminded me of Lonzo, though Lonzo was broader-shouldered, and also a draft dodger. If Lonzo Biggs

52

won a medal, it wouldn't be for fighting. I recalled Lonzo's words back when we were teen-agers, in his beat-up Ford. "Honey, I jus love you too much to use one of them things." And he proceeded to knock me up with Marlene.

Then I remembered that the little girl who sent Lonzo to prison was younger than his oldest daughter. And I asked, "How long have you and Marlene known each other?"

"Met him last week in the men's room," Marlene said, "when I was making my rounds to find which boy would have the best fit."

"Mar-*lene!*" I cried.

Jack Rader turned deep red. "Lord, I don't know, ma'am. Guess somebody should of washed her mouth out with soap. I met Marlene for the first time last week in social studies."

"Mommy, what does she mean?" Bess jumped up and down.

"You're far too young to understand," Jenny said.

"Darn it, Mamma, you're so obvious," Marlene said.

"More talk like that, young lady, and you'll spend the rest of the day upstairs."

"Aw, Mrs. Biggs," Jack said, "she's trying to get a rise. Lord, I've heard ten times worse than anything Marlene can think up. And seen worse."

"You older people are so experienced," Marlene said. I could tell she admired Jack Rader fiercely.

"Ain't much a man don't do in four years over there." Jack shook his head. "I gab about that stuff more'n I ought. But a doc said it's the way to get it out. Whew!"

"He tells some pretty hairy stories, all right," Jenny said.

"Probably nothing a little girl should hear," I said.

"True," Jack agreed. "Awful part is, I had one whooping time tearing off the worst things any mob ever did. Buddies loved it, too. Bothers me." He shook his head. "I ain't a bad person, either. I did real terrible things without one single evil thought in my mind. To make up for it, I otta move into that monastery near Malcolm X and be a monk. The paper which tells how I got my medal"—he stuck his thumb against his nose—"makes me shamed."

"Probably full of gory details," Jenny said.

"When you get out there in the field," Jack went on, "and there really ain't anything evil you can't do, why you feel so free it's wonderful. Some buddies smoked and shot up to get their kicks. Not me. Got mine in action."

"Mamma, it smells like steak," Marlene said.

"I'm hungry," Bess said.

"But I wasn't nothing compared with the South Koreans. Them gooks get one shot from a village, go in and you can't tell which limbs fit where. Men, women, kiddies mixed up in a dern pile. Lord!" He shook his head. "It is one mess."

Marlene looked into the wastebasket. "I see beef bones," she said. "Isn't there anything for Jack and me?"

"Course," Jack Rader was saying, "them gooks worship a different God from us."

"What God is that?" I asked.

"Don't know for sure. But it ain't no god of love. Must be one of them things with a lot of arms and a beak."

"An octopus?" Marlene asked.

"Best thing a guy can do over there, though, is fly one of them jets. That's the top drawer. Free as a bird. And you don't see the mess you're making."

"Mamma's named after Amelia Earhart," Marlene said.

"Marlene, shut your mouth," I told her.

"Only time Grandma Dollarhide read a newspaper," Marlene went on just to sass me, "was before Mamma was born when the Japs shot Amelia Earhart down. 'Farewell to you, Amelia Earhart,'" Marlene sang out, " 'Farewell, First Lady of the Air.'"

"Jack," I said, "you must think the threads got stripped when they screwed this family's heads on."

"Aw, I ain't got any reason to look down on you folks." Jack held his right hand before my face. "See this here?" He made a fist.

"Something's off," I said. "Can't put my finger on it."

"That ain't no thumb," Jack Rader said. "It's a big toe."

Marlene sniggered into her palm.

"Back in Nam," Jack said, "one of my buddies chambered a round a little before he should of. I didn't even know the dang thing was gone till I come to chamber mine. What a whooping power them little rifles got. Just snicked it. So this smart doc sliced the big toe off my right foot and made me a new thumb."

All the king's horses and all the king's men, I thought.

"Maybe he should have cut off your ear," Marlene said. "Made you a new big toe."

"And sticked eyeballs in your ear." Even little Bess had picked up the mood. "Mommy, can I smell it?"

"I'm living on a fruit farm," I said.

"I don't know if fixing up this kind of contraption," said Jack, "is upside down or right side up, and that's the Lord's truth. It's almost like being one of them creatures some brother got off his sister. Well"—he shoved himself up from the table—"I had seconds of meat and taters at Malcolm X." Bending across the table, he gripped my hand between his fingers and his big toe. "Marlene has one good-looking mom. She hadn't of told me, I'd of thought you two was sisters."

"At least let me walk you to the door." Marlene stomped out with him.

"Marlene gives Jack great big kisses!" Bess yelled.

"Now, Bess," Jenny said. "You're going to give Mother the wrong idea."

"Exactly what is the wrong idea, I'd like to know!"

Marlene smirked back in, rotating her bottom like Marilyn Monroe in *Some Like It Hot.* "Where's my T-bone?" But she was acting brazen for a cover-up.

"Jenny, take Bess upstairs."

"Better watch out, Marlene." Jenny took Bess's hand and led her out. "Here it comes."

"Oh, brother," Marlene said. "It's the last time I'll ever bring a boy into this pigsty to meet the family."

"Jack Rader seems like a nice young man," I said, holding my temper. "Isn't he awful old?"

"Mamma, he's twenty-two. I'm sick of going out with boys that look like George Harrison and don't have anything in their skulls but Kung Fu, *Playboy,* and dope."

"Jack Rader's a total hick," I said.

"What about Daddy?"

"Lonzo isn't that much of a hick." I tried to recall my own sweet daddy. Too bad they didn't have Jack Rader's operation around when Daddy was a kid.

"And black is white," said Marlene. "And the ocean's rubber, and—"

"Enough, young lady."

"Jack Rader's the nicest boy I ever met."

"What about the people he shot dead for that medal?"

"I don't care," Marlene said. "It wasn't his fault. It's those old fools in Washington. Why don't you leave me and my boy friends alone and find yourself a man? That's the medicine you need."

"What do you know about such things?"

"Oh, Mamma, I haven't been a—oh!"

Brake lining burned her tongue.

"A what?" A piece worked loose from my heart.

"Nothing," Marlene said.

"What?"

"Damn it to hell!" Marlene chomped her lip. "The kind of head-over-heels example you've given me, it's God's wonder I'm not hustling, or shoplifting, or in the State School for Delinquent Girls. And you sit there gobbling steaks by yourself and have the utter gall—!" She slammed a worn-out loafer against the floor. "Ooh!"

"I know," I said. "You haven't been a virgin so long you can't remember. Isn't that it?"

"If that's the kind of abnormal dirt that stuffs your skull," Marlene shouted, "I don't care what you think!"

She rushed out and pounded upstairs. A door banged.

I sat there feeling older, happier, sorry for Marlene, mixed up, I don't know what, than I ever felt in my life except maybe once. Or twice.

CHAPTER 9

No telling where money's been when it reaches you. A 1951 quarter I once dug from Bess's mouth could have dropped from some filthy wino's trousers into a doggy gutter. And paper money—Lord! Off a scummy whore's mattress, or plucked from the wallet of a suicide three weeks in the drink. Dollars and silver pass more bugs than orgies, but you never dry-clean the stuff. When money's rotten enough, Uncle Sam collects it like garbage and cremates it. Yet there's nothing like cash for cleaning up your life, when it's gotten into a total mess.

So I went upstairs, locked myself in the bathroom, got undressed, peeled the bills off my privates, and while water gushed into my clawfoot bathtub, counted up. There were seven twenty-dollar bills, nine tens, one five, and twenty ones, $255 grand total. Figuring some more, I found myself $381.99 short of what could keep me afloat. Even if those ones had been tens there wouldn't have been enough. But it's peebrained to gripe about windfalls.

Slowly I eased my body into the fiery water. It felt so good to relax and soap myself clean that I hummed, "Since I came to care dum dum for such a millionaire." I needed a millionaire, all right, just so he wasn't fat and smelly. "So I want to tell you, laddy, da da da da da da da swell, that my heart belongs to—"

"Shut up!" Marlene yelled.

Water lapping the tub's rim as I sloshed back to soak, I tried to think good thoughts, like quarry-swimming. And my daddy, who I wished could be visiting, instead of old enema-bag Ethel. Mornings when Daddy and I got up in the shack filled with junk, newspapers, empty tin cans, empty boxes, that Ethel insisted on keeping, we'd stand together at the foot of his bed and pound our socks, stiff with dirt, against the brass. "Softens the dang things up, don't it?" Daddy said, grinning at me out of a crinkled face, flashing his red and blue eyes. "Let's see if them there socks is ready to put on, leetle lady." Like as not, Ethel had spent all night at some honeytonk, Covington's or the Royal Oaks, driving Daddy's seventy-dollar Dodge junk heap with its crank starter, that Ethel called a "nigger car." Her usual excuse was, she'd hit a tent meeting, then hung on with a few calmed-down Holy Rollers to watch Phoebus wake up. "Sure is one fiery ball, that old sonufagun," a baby's sweet smile stretching her little round mouth. Daddy should have blasted Ethel then and there with his Savage twelve-gauge single shot.

Daddy was the ablest person I ever knew, a thick, strong man, who could do anything, though Goldengrove was so backward he almost never found work, and then only as janitor or garbage man. Of course, he did drink wine much too heavily, poor man. He had been a carpenter, fisherman in Maine, termite killer, paperhanger, electrician, and house painter. He taught me how to do plumbing and how to cut a window through solid wall. He could play guitar like Django Rinehart, some of whose fingers were missing, too; sell cars, dig ditches, preach sermons, fix barrels of homemade wine, make rifles and shotguns from scratch, repair any kind of engine, steam, gas, diesel or electric, plow a field, breed and raise any kind of animal, prepare enough barbecue to feed a thousand B.P.O. Elks, and beat any man in a fight, though he was the kindest person I ever knew, and got maimed hand and foot while a medic in World War I But once, when he was a deputy sheriff, he had to kill five men in one night. He'd turn his hunter's eyes and gap-toothed smile on a girl and she'd go hog-wild. After he was dead and couldn't take his part, Ethel told me how young men and women would show up looking for Daddy—their mothers confessed he was their real father. "Your mamma's better'n you might think," Casey once said, me on his lap. "Want the truth, I ain't treated Ethel worth shit." Blind love never fixed his arrow into a more unfortunate heart.

After World War I, Daddy was third mate on Cornelius Whittaker III's yacht that sailed the seven seas hooking from the depths sea monsters nobody knew existed. "It was night and moonless," Daddy told me. "We done dropped anchor over the Mariana Trench, seven miles deep. Loafin on the stern by my lonesome lookin at the still water, I seen this leetle bright speck, star-reflection I thought, but it kept growin bigger. Couldn't stop lookin to save my soul, that leetle dot puffin up to egg size, cat size, cow size, elephant size, till the dang thing's bigger'n a steam engine, with giant tentacles. Then whoosh! up pop these giant eyes like bonfires burnin into mine. I seen this white beak, twice bigger'n me, mongst them thick, white arms. Sane man would of howled back to his bunk. But I wait for that thing to reach up and gather me to its hole, cause I was tempted to dive down. Lord, take me in your arms. For the hell of it, I reach in my pocket and toss this leetle Jap yen tween them dang eyes. Sea turns black. Thing's gone like shit off a shovel, water lickin the side of Whittaker's yacht. Course, she wasn't but a giant squid flyin out of her depth. Miracle the pressure change didn't blow her to bits, which is how come I'm the only man in God's creation who ever saw one of them monsters live and whole."

Oh, Daddy. If you hadn't needed to die, a few bumps in my life would have ironed out. If only you hadn't run off when I was fourteen and knocked up. They knew it was your body by the hands and feet only.

Then, in the tub, I found myself trying again to remember that other thing, down there, I knew, like the squid, but never surfacing no matter how I dredged for it.

Soaking, thinking only of my comfort, suddenly I knew what a selfish mother I was to my girls, no better than Ethel after Daddy left. I pulled the plug, ran to my room, stuffed the money in my nightstand, pulled my robe on, then ran downstairs and bedded three T-bones under the broiler. When they were rare, I called, "Kids!"

Bess came first.

"Where've you girls been?"

"Marlene's room," Bess said. "Poor Marlene."

Jenny came in. "Yum," she said.

"Take a steak to Marlene," I said, "and eat one yourself."

"I love to smell meat," Bess said, digging into the juicy pieces I sliced for her.

It had been one hellish day. Taking the paper off my porch, I settled on my ragged living-room sofa by the brick fireplace we never used, and treated myself to the news. It looked like the whole world had flying elbows. A convicted rapist murdered two guards and escaped from the Illinois pen. In Indiana, a fourteen-year-old girl had been raped and murdered by her stepfather, who barricaded himself in their home and finally blew his brains out. A hurricane was breaking up Cuba, spearing sugar stalks through phone poles. Doctors were under investigation for experimenting with live aborted fetuses. So many rapist-murderers worked overtime, it was a wonder enough honest citizens remained to play victim. Crocodiles ate Hindus in the Ganges. Two babysitters found a young woman, wearing shorts and halter, rock-hard in a deepfreeze, bullet through her temple. And an archbishop declared that celibacy among the priesthood was keeping God alive and fresh, thank you kindly.

As usual, local news featured the Cat Burglar, who had struck a downtown toy shop the night before, slipping in and out through a narrow basement window and making off with $6.57 in change. The poor bastard needed a manager. In ten break-ins, the most the nut ever got at one time was ten bucks from a billfold in Macy's lost and found, hardly enough to finance the poems left behind. The new prize-winner, scrawled in a child's printing, read:

$6.57
Won't send me to heaven,
I'm real disappointed, and how.
But fall's not my season,
That must be the reason,
So hail, farewell, and meow.

                              Cat Burglar

   This tumbler of pee recalled my lit class that night at the
university. But Lord, I was weary. And my raving young
teacher wouldn't miss me. Once he got going, he forgot other
people were in the room, like a crazy man abusing himself.
   My relationship with school always had been weird.
There was a time in high school, before I got pregnant and
went haywire and the authorities sent me up, that I earned
straight A's, got elected student council treasurer and president of Tri-Y. At the start of my sophomore year, I was the
most popular girl in Goldengrove High School, which made
the snotty clique of rich town girls resentful. Their daddies
owned stonemills, the Olds agency, Alden's department
store, Walgreen's and the Roxy. But it didn't mean catpoop
compared with endowments which are only nature's to give.
   On the other hand, I liked grade school as little as reform
school later on. An old bitch in first grade cracked my
knuckles with a rattan all the time for no reason. One Saturday morning, I found a kitchen match in the gutter, ran
straight to a part of the school shielded by steps, struck the
match, and held it against a brick on the schoolhouse wall.
Which shows they weren't teaching me anything, either.
Later on, of course, I learned better.
   I decided to cut night class, no great to-do, especially
since I noticed that car thieves the day before had swiped ten
autos parked on campus. The book on the docket was that
pervert's fantasy that every woman in Paris was hot to
impale herself on his prong. And because I just knew the
author would stop at nothing, even something totally repul-

sive as incest, my bearded boy would bump and grind like Rose la Rose. "What does that *mean?*" he'd often ask. "God, reality reeks with meaning. Look how it all hangs together!" Sure it does. Depending on what book he was pummeling us with, he was as likely to spray out, "There's no order, except sheer accident, or what we put there ourselves!" Or, "Nature's loaded with order and meaning, chaos is in man's eyes." I took careful notes, though in grading our exams, he seemed to forget what he'd said.

It was dark out. A white, dead glow reached from the dining room, where the TV crackled with phony laughter, then sang out, "If you believe in Peanut Butter, you gotta believe in—" I roused myself from the couch and wandered onto the porch. Winter was coming, a chilly breeze that blew gently down from outer space, leaving me almost helpless with its feathery touching. No moon. The stars burned like matches. Werewolves and vampires could have themselves a sound sleep, something I sorely needed, and I went back inside, first tossing the evening paper on top of trash that filled an uncovered barrel.

Jenny and Bess lay belly down before the TV.

"School tomorrow," I said.

"It's the real thi-ing," whinnied the TV as I snuffed it out.

"Come on, Mother," Jenny said. "I want to know what happens next."

"No arguing. Upstairs!"

"Tuck me in, Mommy," said Bess.

I did. And tucked in Jenny, too, though the poor thing outweighed me by twenty pounds.

On the way to my room, I passed Marlene's shut door. Her plate lay outside, T-bone gnawed clean. I almost knocked, but kept going to my room. Shucking my robe, I crawled between the sheets and thought of those dollars beside Joe Palooka's middle finger. Maybe, just maybe, I could help spring Lonzo Biggs from the pen. At the very least, I could go out and buy some cream to keep looking young. Money relaxes you more than any sleeping pill.

I stood outside our locked bathroom door and yelled, "Lord, Errol, what takes you so long in there?"

"German Lugers, goddamn it!" Errol shouted. "I always think about German Lugers when I'm taking a crap!"

"But our baby's in the yard eating her own poop!" I called.

"So don't disturb me when I'm reading," Errol said in a snotty voice. "You don't like to be disturbed when you're reading."

A hand touched my body. There stood Joy Silverspring, naked and bony, pulling a shape down from the wound between her legs. It was greasy, like a squirrel's skinned carcass. Joy said, "Thought you'd like to see your wickedness, Mrs. Shiflet-Biggs. Not that it's any of my business." The carcass writhed on my floor, opened its pink eyes and mewed something about Joy she didn't have the slightest knowledge of herself. Then I noticed that I was barenaked, too. At the foot of the steps stood Jack Rader. "Your nose is the God of love," he said, as if I had asked the time. "When you blow your nose, that's God's voice." Something shaggy pinned me helpless against a stone ledge. "Love your dang butt," the thing panted. "Sure ain't stopping now." "Mamma!" Marlene cried from the yard. "Lookit this!" "Yes, Marlene!" I shouted. "The inchworm is having a great time in your Dixie cup!"

"Maria?"

I was flying or floating. Black ink painted my eyeballs. Something awful was going on.

"It's your wicked man, Mother," whispered a voice.

"You the Cat Burglar?" I asked.

"His disciple. We humans are profound imitators." The stench of wine was on his breath. "If he can enjoy his outrages, why can't I?"

"There's no money in the house."

"I wonder, then. What would you call that crisp paper I stole from your nightstand?" Then he asked, Did I like this? Was that all right? "Just making sure you get your money's worth," he added considerately. "Render unto Caesar."

I gouged my nails into his damned back. "I need that money to feed my children."

"Lucky thing my calling keeps me swaddled," he whispered. "I'm being crucified for my sins."

"You must have busted out of the loony bin," I gasped, in terror of my life and my girls'.

"Just your run-of-the-mill repressed killer," he said.

"Are you going to murder me, too?"

"Only brought a blunt instrument along, Amelia, ha ha."

"You bastard. It's a terrible thing you're making me do."

"This bastard'll pay in hell," he whispered, blowing wine in my face. "So I took an offering this evening to grease the hot palm of Mammon."

"Shift your hairy rib bones."

"The shirt of penance, lady."

Humiliated, I started sobbing against this maniac who held me like a vise.

"There, child." He petted my shoulder. "I'm an evil daddy-o."

"You son of a bitch," I sobbed.

"True, I am that," he whispered calmly. Then, "Call it a dream, Mother. Pretend it never happened." Sheets rustled, the mattress jumped. Starchy clothes crackled. "Sleepy-bye."

I heard the rapist shipleg down the stairs. The front door shut. Feet rattled the porch.

I must have fainted from terror—only to wake frantic, gray light weeping like pus around my blind. I checked the nightstand drawer. The money was gone, all of it. Rushing to the bathroom, crouching like a lunatic in the tub, I piped vinegar into my wounded innards.

I was toweling myself when someone pounded the front door. "Cops," I thought. "Errol Shiflet's turned me in. Well, let's take the worst when it comes." I threw on my robe, stumbled downstairs, and opened the door.

But it wasn't law and order. On the porch stood old Ethel, smiling blissfully, toothless like a newborn infant.

CHAPTER *10*

With one sly look-round, Ethel took in the mess of my living room. "Seems like you been too busy makin your own bed to ever lie down in it," she said.

We didn't touch each other, though we hadn't met for six years, when I was divorcing Errol for committing adultery with a dozen coeds. Marlene had been ten, and Jenny only six. Ethel had come then, she said, to haul me through yet another disorderly period in my life. But her idea of help consisted of gobbling all food in the house, no doubt to reduce clutter. Since it took Errol weeks to float his pets out, she once caught a large angelfish, filleted it, and flopped it into a sandwich, with pickle relish and mayonnaise. "Woman gets to craving a little strange," she'd leered, "just like a man." Every time the girls looked peaked, which was often during that ungodly mess, she'd say, "Y'uns need a enema. C'mon, let old Ethel launder your innards." Errol later told me that when he returned for his tanks, Ethel greeted him wearing a see-through nightie. Wouldn't he like to fish her pond instead? she asked. "I'd have had to strap my ankles to the bedpost," Errol had laughed. Since nothing was sacred to Ethel, she finally took a crack at Lonzo, who I'd already decided to marry a second time. "Horny old sow," Lonzo laughed when he told me. "Good thing she never had a son, he'd of been screwed fifty different ways till Sunday before he ever hit fourteen."

Now Ethel said, "Casey always did try and coach you on neatness. Looks like you got more of your old mom floatin round than your pa ever managed to get in, he he. Well, what's past is dead. Looks like me and you got enough present to patch up, without worryin a old account."

"When did your bus get in?" I asked.

"Aw, sweetie, your old mom travels in style." She snapped up a living-room blind. "Looky."

"What on earth is that?"

" '67 LTD," Ethel said. "We'uns can maybe get six hundred cash, dependin on how slick I can make a deal." Gray morning washed over her wrinkled orange tent of a dress, short gray hair in bad need of cleaning, smooth broad face. Aiming her red peehole eyes into mine, she showed her pink gums. "There's more goodies inside," Ethel said.

"Where'd you get that car? From your peach?"

"He he. Ethel just drove a thousand miles in one hop, green lights all the way. She's hungry. Any weenies an beansie-weensies in the house? Let's hit the kitchen." She hustled ahead of me with that bouncy walk she kept all her life, yanked the icebox open, and pawed inside the freezing compartment. "Sweetie, done found me a T-bone. How come you never said nothin bout it?"

"Can you gum through steak?" I asked.

"Your mamma can gum steel," Ethel said. "Ain't nothin I love more'n a tore-down mess."

"You've been living one all your life."

"He he, I'm a tough old bird, I am. Let's cook up this here meat, sweetie."

She warmed it bleeding rare, and with my rusty butcher knife halved the slab cockeyed, so if the two pieces had been weighed in the scales of justice, that arm wouldn't have moved an inch up or down. Even blood puddles on our plates looked the same. Ethel and I plunged in knives and forks, ate fast and silent, finished at the same time. "Takes more'n that to fill me," Ethel said. "Do I see a lard can in that cupboard?" She reached it down and forked white gunk into her mouth.

"Best old stuff for stoppin babies," she gasped between

chomps. "Whenever Casey's eyes fired that gleam, it was quick to the lard can and a gob up the old baby factory. No accidents. Course, them docs carved out my plumbin years back. Should of used this goo yourself four times in the past, hey?"

"You coached me well, Mamma." I remembered crud I should erase for good.

"That old flyin dentist, wasn't he a peach?" Ethel dropped her fork and clapped her small fat hands. "All them Mason jars of cash buried under his yard. Sweetie, you surely was at your best on that job!"

"Got me the honor of two years in reform school, after you left me holding the bag."

"But wasn't it fun? Up there in that little contraption of his on top of the world? Shitfire, everbody could have a ball if they let themselves go!"

"The revenge part was fun," I said. "Before I had to pay the piper." Then I laughed, because the flying dentist's airplane was a Piper.

"Oh, sweetie, your old mom likes seein your sad face flit away. You was lookin guilty. Shee-it! Guilt ain't worth a lighted fart. It's what killed off Casey Dollarhide. Revenge —now that's a much nicer feelin than guilt, ain't it?" Through the orange cloth, Ethel suddenly grabbed her guts. "Oh! Ooh!"

"What is it, Mamma?"

"Buster's pecker must of gone in too far." Ethel's reflection grimaced up from the blood on her plate. Sudden as the pain hit, it seemed to leave, and she sat straight. "Whew! Before them little grandkids of mine wake up, let's us bounce outside and see Santy Claus."

I found the first coat at hand, Marlene's, pulled it on over my robe, and stuck my bare feet into a pair of Jenny's galoshes. "Aren't you cold?" I asked.

"Naw. This blubber warms me in dead winter."

The morning smelled like smokestacks. My eyes watered, my nose filled. Through the windows of that yellow car, I saw stacked newspapers, magazines, shoeboxes tied with string,

bundles of greasy rags, one brown sack stuffed to blowup
with folded sacks. On the dash lay wadded Kleenex, men's
sunglasses snapped at the bridge, a sock knotted like a rubber
rotting on a country road. There was a brown apple core, and
a sandwich crust, which surprised me, since Ethel usually ate
everything, seeds and stem.

"You brought that load of junk a thousand miles?" I
asked.

"Never know when a sack or rag's gonna come in handy,
sweetie." She opened a back-seat door. Newspapers flopped
to the gutter. "Shitfire!" Ethel grunted. "Them is good as
cash. Help here. Ain't spry like I was."

"I don't need old papers."

"Just reach under the back seat, sweetie."

I hauled a packed gunnysack onto the scraggly curbside
grass.

"Don't open the dern thing out here," Ethel said.

"What's in it, Mamma? Tell me."

Ethel smiled like Grandma Rat. "Taters, honeypie.
Weenies an beansie-weensies, he he. Horn o Plenty."

I gathered an armload of fallen newspaper to stuff back
into the LTD.

"Might as well cart all this honey into the hive," Ethel
said, dragging her gunnysack to the porch.

"Mamma, my house is messy enough without your junk."

"One more gob o spit in a sewer, darlin."

Marlene, Jenny, and Bess waited inside the door. "Ain't
you the loveliest sight!" their grandma sighed. The night-
gowns Jenny and Bess had on were shapeless flannel sacks,
but Marlene wore a short red nightie that showed all.
"Marlene, how you have growed!"

"So have you, Grandma," Marlene said.

"Your grandma drove a thousand miles to see you girls." I
looked hard at Marlene. "She doesn't need any wise-assing."

"Lemme gather some big hugs all round," Ethel said.

When I pitched my armload of newspaper splat into the
living room, dust poofed up.

"Who's this here weenie thing?" Laying her sack by,
Ethel made for Bess.

"Bess," I said, "give Grandma a big hug."

"You're fat," Bess said.

"Oh Lord, honey, ain't it the truth?" Ethel whooshed Bess off the floor. She pressed the child between her huge, blubbery boobs.

"You stink," Bess said.

"Sweet Jesus." Ethel set Bess down fast. "Maybe I ain't never lived the way a body should." Tears formed in Ethel's tiny red eyes.

"Hello there, Grandmother," Jenny said slowly. "It's good to see you again."

"Jenny," Ethel said. "Don't you an me need to drop a couple pounds?"

"If you say so, Grandmother."

"Anymore, I don't know what to say." Ethel looked like some vandal had slashed her tires.

Then her eyes narrowed and she was her ornery self again. "Amelia, that little un looks peaked. She needs a enema."

"Maybe you need one yourself," I shot back.

"Now that big Marlene." Ethel's eyes widened like a snake's mouth. "She looks just downright fine!"

"Fine for what, Grandma?" Marlene asked.

"Any little old job you got in mind, sweetie," Ethel said.

"I'm an innocent schoolgirl," Marlene said.

"Way I hear it, there ain't no such thing anymore." Ethel drilled Marlene with those small, red eyes. "I know you young girls, he he. Ethel knows what goes on in those pointy heads. *Wicked* things!" She smacked her small hands together. "Plain wicked! Right now, this very second, you're thinkin wicked thoughts! Hey? Ain't I right? Old Ethel knows!"

Marlene hung for dear life onto a brazen stare. Then she fidgeted, crossed her hands over her crotch, blinked and looked at the floor, the first time I saw anyone stare her down.

"He he he," went Ethel.

"I was thinking"—Marlene hesitated—"wondering, like maybe, uh, what's for breakfast?"

"Breakfast?" Now Ethel fastened her stare onto Jenny. "Looks like somebody been gettin too dang much breakfast! Maybe somebody better drop some flab." She paused. "If she's gonna be useful roun this setup."

"You mean, pull my own weight, Grandmother?" Jenny asked, with the blandest look in the world.

"He he. Don't misjudge this middle child." Ethel tapped her own temple. "Slim her down, we got ourselves one slick number."

"Never wanted a girls' softball team," I said.

"How bout a girls' hardball team?" Ethel leered.

"All of you, get your clothes on," I said.

Bess scooted upstairs. Jenny gave Ethel a big hug. "Thanks, big darlin," Ethel murmured. Marlene hesitated. Then she, too, hugged Ethel and followed Jenny up.

"I love money so much it'd be slick to squat and give birth to it," Ethel threw in out of left field.

"What about giving birth to a fin, so I can send Marlene to the store. You and I ate the last food."

Ethel fished down the neck of her orange puptent, rummaged in her bra, and came up with a small roll of bills, from which she peeled a fiver. "I'll give Marlene this. Now haul that gunnysack to your room."

I did, and tossed it on my mussed bed, over a stain in the sheet.

Downstairs, Marlene was dressed, as usual in something that made a figleaf look like a formal gown. Ethel handed her the bill and told her to get something for breakfast.

"This thing real?" Marlene asked, knowing that her grandma had been hauled in more than once for counterfeiting.

"What you don't know," Ethel said, "the pigs can't third-degree loose."

After Marlene had gone, Ethel said, "That there is one hot number. Lucky you ain't got no man in this sty. He might yield to temptation."

"Mamma, you have got the filthiest mind on this planet."

"This here's one filthy dang planet," Ethel said. "Smell its breath out there? Let's me an you unload the wagon."

"Old greasy rags? Let's open the bag first."

"Wait till Christmas. C'mon. There's more outside than you think."

In Marlene's coat and Jenny's unsnapped galoshes I followed Ethel out. She swung open the tailgate, and rummaged shoulder-deep in the trash's bowels. At last she pulled out a long black case, and handed it to me. "This here's a start."

It was nearly 7:30. House doors slammed, cars ground to a start. I started to unzip the case. "Hold on there, eagerness," Ethel said. "Don't want none of your neighbors seein that thing. Place sure is crawlin with darkies. Ever had one of them big rods stuck up in you, sweetie? He he."

I ignored her dirt. "What's here?"

"Ithaca shotgun, worth a hunnerd. With a slick deal, I can clear twenty. Like the gun old Sam Walters back on Pigeon Hill blasted his darlin daughter Samantha and himself with. After he knocked her up. Yep. Sure is good old Lonzo ain't round no more." She winked one watery red eye at me. Sun bleered through the smog. "Course, sweetie, this here's just appetizers. Once you run that red light, ain't no reason not to go all out."

"Will it be like old times, Mamma? Back when I miscarried and went hog-wild?"

"If that's what you want," Ethel said. "Now les tap that sack of goodies." On the porch, she stopped by my garbage cans and plucked out the newspaper I'd tossed the night before. "Shitfire, old papers're worth five, ten bucks a year. Hey, know this Cat Burglar?"

"Why should I?"

"Sometimes," she muttered, "the real pros know each other." Resting the shotgun against my couch, she read the article. "But this dumbass ain't no pro," she said, disgusted. "Looks like all he wants is get himself caught. Who'd pull such a goatfuck trick?"

"Errol Shiflet," I answered, before even thinking. "He always works bassackward."

"Old Errol?" Ethel cried out with glee. "That wonderful shithead?"

71

I said, "Didn't he have his students break into a radio station? Mainly he wants to devil his old man, who's flying in any day now. It's old home week in Elm City."

"He's a doc, ain't he? Don't that mean he's loaded?"

"He's a tightwad."

"Done forgot the ropes?" Ethel asked. "Ain't he married to a bitch? And ain't he scared shitless of her like most educated fools? It sure don't hurt none to think ahead. Remember that flying dentist? Honey, you brung that off so slick it sent shivers through me."

Hugging a grocery sack, Marlene swung past.

"That there fin pass the grocer?" Ethel grinned.

"Sure," said Marlene. "Gorgeous George was too busy eyeing me to check out your graphics." She headed into the kitchen and started clanking dishes.

"Let's get upstairs," I said.

"Can't wait to open that bag, can you, baby daughter?"

It was true. For some reason, I felt like the cast-iron water heater in the kitchen of that Congress Avenue rattrap in Goldengrove, where Lonzo and I lived the first time we got married. You twisted the gas and lit the grid with a match. Woe to anyone who fired that blowtorch and forgot, because the contraption could blast sky-high. When once I did forget till almost too late, I stopped the gas and rushed to turn on all three hot water faucets. For fifteen minutes they gushed pure steam, till the apartment was cottony with fog, and windowpanes ran solid water. The fire was burning underneath me now, with nobody to open my taps.

"That's my egg!" Bess yelled. Something crashed in the kitchen. Hunks of glass scattered.

"It's your fault!" Marlene shouted.

"Mamma," I pleaded, "before I explode!"

The trip upstairs left Ethel wheezing. "Empty er out," she gasped, flopping on the bed beside the bag, clutching her belly. "I done split a stitch."

Propping the shotgun inside my closet, I said, "You all right, Mamma?"

"I'm tore in two opposite directions, don't you know. It's mighty hard bein your—" She didn't finish.

I untied the gunnysack, and dumped Christmas beside Ethel on my stained mattress. A half-dozen credit cards clickety-clacked. There lay a Timex pocket watch, a thick Masonic ring, zircon blinking. False teeth, uppers and lowers, grinned near each other. There were two earplugs, a greenish metal crucifix, a little padlock key on a paper clip, a bar of ersatz chocolate melted shapeless in its wrapper, a can of Maine sardines, the Book of Mormon, a leather pouch that felt like it weighed a pound, full of gold teeth which, Ethel told me, Charlie had yanked from dead Japs on Guam, a palm-size automatic pistol with exposed hammer, a roll of green toilet paper, a fat manilla envelope scrawled, "Taxes, 1968–70," a twelve-pack of lubricated Trojans, a conch large enough to hide the cows it called home, a fifth of California chianti, a new Kennedy half dollar, minted from tin rather than silver, a birth certificate for Charles Roger Peen, born September 1, 1914, an eight-page Bible featuring Daisy Mae and Popeye, a crinkled blessing supposedly from Pope Pius XII, a rabbit's foot, and a postcard of Winged Victory, a headless statue in Paris, France. There was also a small, thick packet, brown paper held together with Scotch tape. It was like ripping open a shark's belly.

"Whose stuff is all this, Mamma?"

"Charlie," Ethel wheezed. "Car, too. Cleaned out the coldass sonumbitch. Got bout a hunnerd dollars real cash, too. Anybody steps in my way's gonna get coldcocked if it takes me forever. Anybody!"

"Aren't the cops chasing you down?"

"No." Ethel blinked at the puddle of loot and junk. "Because of that tax stuff. Charlie's been cheating Uncle Sam blind for years. Proof's there." She tapped the envelope. "Cops land me, I bury Charlie in the pen. I ain't one to let a old account go unsettled."

"What's in here?" I tore open the thick brown packet and found a green Ben Franklin staring up at me. "Jesus Christ."

"Ben goes clear to the bottom," Ethel said. "A whole damn ream. Five hundred deep. Randy old Ben fathered bastards all over the place, didn't he?"

"Fifty thousand dollars?"

"Fake," Ethel said. "Me, Charlie and Buster done made him ourselves. Still, it looks real and feels tough and crisp, don't it. That there's fine rag paper."

Everything seemed so weird and unreal. I thought of Lonzo in the slammer, then of what hit me on this same mattress in the dead of last night, and it spooked me so that before I knew it, I heaved myself on Ethel's bosom. We glommed together like Siamese twins.

"Shitfire," Mamma blubbered.

"Shitfire."

"By the stone-cold Christ," Mamma sobbed, "while there's time left, honey, we'uns gonna have us one grand toot!"

CHAPTER *11*

After the kids got off to school, Ethel and I transfused junk from Charlie's yellow chariot into my old brown house.

"Should be pumping ship," I said, "instead of sucking in bilge."

"Everthing's got value," Ethel said. "It's my religious practice to not throw nothin out. Y'uns use this fireplace?"

"With wood thirty-three bucks a cord?"

"Fine for newspapers, an that there sack o sweeperbags."

Used disposable bags these were, gray mungpuffs bulging from their cardboard faces. "Lord God," I moaned, and tossed them in the living-room fireplace, which already stank of damp soot and mold.

"If you must use them bags, finger the hole an work the guck out," Ethel explained. "Next, honey, I gotta buy me some henna an go on the warpath."

"Buy it?" I threw back. "Mamma, you're slipping."

"Wheee-hah!" A cry of glee. "Limber up them fingers, sweetie pie. If the world chops away our beauty by the hunk, we sure got a right to steal."

"Is there a crime on God's earth you can't justify?"

She winked a red eye. "I'm a criminal genius, I am."

I'd almost forgotten how natural stealing was. It's a craft—look ahead and adjust to whatever comes up. Some think law is a stone, solid and heavy, whether or not a cop's around. Say you've stopped for a red light on an empty road, no sheriff in sight, your dearest relative in the car bleeding to death, and the nearest hospital five miles off. Some fools would hold for green, red blood flying, because "law" is hovering in the sky like a silent eyeball. Nature's laws are real without cops, but not human laws, unless you crack down on yourself, which is criminal when you're bleeding to death. So I put on a blue and white tweed coat with large pockets. Ethel washed herself, so she didn't smell so ornery, but all she had to wear was that orange puptent. Climbing behind the LTD's wheel, I said, "Let me handle this, Mamma. They'd arrest you for breaking the ray that opens the door."

"Honey, run this show any way you like." Ethel settled back in her seat. "I may retire from active duty here on out and just supervise."

I drove to downtown Elm City where the air smelled like the roaring hind end of a bus, and parked on the Green, across from the police station, a four-story brick building. The Green is a grass square, four blocks on a side. Stainless steel lightposts stand guard all round it, and three ancient churches wart its middle. Three hundred years ago, when typhoid wiped out half the first settlers, survivors dug a mass grave in the Green. Last time a hurricane blew down a big oak, human skeletons were tangled in its roots. Legend says when Gabriel toots his trumpet, all forty thousand Elect will hunker like buzzards on the Green's southeast corner, then flap to heaven in a black swarm.

Across the Green's far side stands Elm City University, like a real monastery, all cloistered and gargoyled.

"Wait here." I climbed out.

"You're boss now, honey."

The Green boiled with pigeons, so graceful coming in to land, then fat and jerky on the ground, shuffling, looking off at nothing in particular. Winos sprawled on benches. I seldom walked through the Green, they said such terrible things to me.

I jaywalked to a Liggett's Pharmacy, gleaming with

chrome and glass. Three other shoppers were in the store, one checkout register of six was open, and the druggist was counting pills. The biggest crooks in any store are its employees, who love to nail shoplifters out of sheer hypocrisy. A pair of TV cameras near the ceiling panned back and forth, but where's the fun without risk? Picking a box of Cracker Jack, I held it in plain sight, then made for the cosmetics aisle, where I found my wrinkle grease. It so pissed me off that the price had jumped a buck to $8.50, I palmed five jars into my pocket, headed for the hair aisle, swiped a pack of Dust Red, marched to the register with Charlie's small roll for a shield, dug up a sawbuck for the Cracker Jack, collected my change, and breezed out.

I threw some Cracker Jack on the pavement, and pigeons scratched after it like fingernails. "Eat up, sweethearts." Then my fingers hit cellophane, and I pulled out the prize, a cheapo ring. Both band and emerald were genuine plastic, but my spirits were soaring like I'd sniffed glue, and I slipped the prize onto my heart finger.

In the car, Ethel leaned forward squeezing her guts with both hands.

"Mamma, I'm back in the saddle again!"

"Ooooh," she groaned, then pulled herself slowly up and stared out the bug-splattered windshield at nothing. "How come we're wastin energy on peanuts, like that dang Cat Burglar?" she asked.

"See my ring?"

"Lordy, child, how old are you, fourteen?"

I steered the powerful car from the curb. The first light was green and I sailed through, and through the yellow on the second light. "Mamma, aren't we gonna need the phone?"

"Phone's a must."

Cars screeched to a honking stop as I sailed, elbows flying, through a red light. Bell Telephone was a half mile from the Green, an eight-story checkerboard of sky-blue panels and glass. I whipped the LTD neatly into a parking space reserved for Mr. Ghostly, Second Vice-President, grabbed up the open Cracker Jack box, and said, "Be gone a split second."

"I'd think you was Frankenstein," Ethel said, "if you wasn't so cutesy-wootsy."

Inside were white walls, white floors, white light, and the stink of ashtrays. A dozen people stood lined up before a cashier's bars. I shoved in at the front and asked, "Where's Becky Willett?"

"Wait your turn!" snorted a fat man behind me.

"Hold your horses, Jasper," I said. "I'm helping you stay rich a few more seconds."

"She's a service representative," said the cashier, a sallow girl who didn't look up. "First door on your left."

"Generation of vipers," the fat man muttered.

I entered an enormous room, with ceiling-high windows looking out on sidewalk, parking meters, and a boarded-up auto-fixit across the street. Desks stood in rows, like an overgrown schoolroom. Near the middle I spotted Becky Willett's nameplate. "Ho there, Becky!" I yelled.

She looked at me, along with everyone else, a cute child with stringy, straw-blond hair and pale skin. "Help you?"

"Honey, I'm Amelia Biggs."

"Any more dirty phone calls?" She flashed a little grin.

"Becky, I could tell you things that'd pop your eardrums. But here's a present." I plunked the Cracker Jack on her blotter.

"What's the big disturbance here?" A young man had walked up. He had a baby face, pug nose, and a little round mouth I expected to drool Pablum.

"Supervisor," whispered Becky Willett.

"This fool the coffee drinker you told me about?" I asked.

"What on earth—" he began.

"Is this a sweatshop?" I said. "Who spends all day swilling coffee while others work, right, Becky?"

"When you finish gossiping with this loudmouth friend of yours," he told her, "you are fired." He stomped off. Several women sat with a smack.

78

"What happened?" Becky Willett asked.

"That piss-ant fired you. But it's clearly for the best."

She flicked at the Cracker Jack box. "Gee. I lost my job."

"Here." I dug the last of Charlie's cash from my coat pocket, and peeled off three double sawbucks, a sawbuck and a fin. "Take the phone out of this and keep the change for yourself." That left me with a few singles and some silver.

"Sure. Sure thing," she murmured.

"Got to run," I said. "Maybe I'll come back tonight and burn this joint down."

By the time Marlene, Jenny, and Bess got home, Ethel had dyed her ragmop red and stuck in her teeth. "Dumb to lose a good contact cause he's persnickety," she said.

"Why, Grandma," said Marlene, "what big teeth you have."

"Ain't et a young girl in days," Ethel growled.

Jenny said, "Grandmother, you'll be happy to know that I didn't eat lunch."

"Wonderful, darlin. You're *my* girl, ain't you! A few good enemas to hurry things, you'll get down to fightin trim."

"Are you still my grandma?" Bess asked. "You smell like her."

That night, Ethel asked, "Is the Post Road like it was last I come here?"

"Ugly as ever," I said.

"Pigs busted up them honkeytonks?"

"Cruise round, Mamma. You'll find plenty of scabs to pick, and under every one, a running sore."

"Wonderful to know the years don't change everthing. Looky, gimme whatever dough's left and I'll get started."

I straightened the few crumpled ones and laid them in her palm. "Lord Jesus," Ethel murmured. "You need a keeper, don't you."

She took off in the LTD.

Two minutes later Jack Rader banged politely on my kitchen door, came in, and shook my hand between his fingers and big toe. "When I come up," he said, "I seen the sweetest yellow wagon driving away."

"Mamma," I said.

"Grandma makes me wonder," said Marlene, prancing into the kitchen, "if maternity is uncertain like paternity. I keep hoping Grandma Dollarhide, or whatever her name is now—"

"Think maybe it's Peen," I said.

"—got bypassed when Mother Nature was working her slow way up to me. Come on, Jack. Let's track down a filthy movie."

"This is a school night," I told her.

"Mamma," Marlene said, "you have the most mixed-up values of anyone."

"Shoot, Marlene, quit that stuff," scolded Jack Rader. "Mrs. Biggs, I'll see she ain't out past her bedtime." Holding hands, or whatever, they galloped into the darkness.

I was settling down with that unnatural book by the aging adolescent in Paris, frantically busy burying his dong, when the kitchen phone rang. Errol Shiflet, Ph.D., got right to the point. "Don't you have a head on your shoulders?"

"Naughty Errol," taunted a background voice.

"They accuse me of stealing Bill's money, Amelia. And wrecking their cars after they split to an orgy. Bill's threatening to dump Clorox on my Red Devil. And it's all your doing."

"I do not," I said, "have one cent belonging to that idiot."

"Lord, your criminal past's welling up," Errol groaned.

"So what do you rake in on your nightly tomcatting around town?"

"You must have something in mind, Christ knows what."

"For one thing, that radio station you burglarized. You'd do anything to humiliate your old man."

"That prick flew in alone last night. He's staying with rich friends near the Maltby Lakes and girding his limp loins to rip open his son's throat again. Look, would you hire out your ball-cutting talents? I'll provide rusty corkscrews and dull knives."

"I'm sick of your insults," I said. But I couldn't help feeling sorry for the diseased creature, who I once loved till I found he had less self-control than a wino with DT's.

"There's one woman, at least, who cares about me," Errol said.

"That stuck-up redhead?"

"No. A mature woman, who knows what a mature man needs."

"Errol, you can't cure clap by giving it to somebody else!" And I slammed down the phone. Seconds later, it jangled again. "Errol, I've had enough crap for a lifetime!" I shouted into the receiver.

"Errol Flynn?" replied a repulsively familiar and chipper voice. "Wrong bad actor. Guess again."

"What do you want now?"

"Anything I can get. No hard feelings last night, I hope, ha ha."

"Listen to me, Jasper—"

"James Dean's the winning answer. Remember? Come and get your pretty prize."

"—if you try to pull that stunt again—"

"But definitely. I've deprived myself too long, dear."

"—I'll shoot holes through your damn pinhead, you degenerate thief!"

"Oh, thanks, Mother, for a pat on my deformed soul. I'll burn candles to you in perpetuity."

He sounded so hopelessly crazy I felt my fury beginning to dim. "Well, you've been warned."

"I'm an imp of the perverse," he babbled. "Warnings only drive po me to plumb new depths."

"Maybe you'll do the world a service," I said, "and drown in them."

I hung up, then lifted the phone off its hook. The black monster hummed awhile, beeped noisily for a minute, and at last went dead. Staggering into the living room, I passed out on the couch.

CHAPTER *12*

I lay in the beat-up crib which had been mine, then Marlene's, Jenny's, and Bess's. But its bars were thick-frosted and steaming with cold. I wore only a full suit of goosepimples. Snakes and huge spiders rustled against the floorboards, and I thought, "Amelia, what a fix. Freeze solid, or jump out and get gobbled." Then I opened my eyes to find myself lying on the couch, filthy novel open in my lap, Cracker Jack ring on my wedding finger and the front door wide open sucking in cold night air. But it was no relief to see Ethel's plastic grin in the doorway, or the mussed, ragged creature beside her.

"Hi, sweetchips," he said. "Got a bah-ul in the house?"

"A whah-ul?" I asked.

"Bottle," Ethel said. "Ain't that how Elm City talks?"

"You promised a bah-ul," the man told Ethel.

"Ain't the main reason you come, is it, sweetie?" Standing her hippo bulk tiptoe, Ethel tweaked his gray and wrinkled cheeks. The man could have been sixty, eighty, even forty. I thought of jail cells, honkeytonks, gutters, needles, barfights, bug-ridden one-night stands.

"Should of stopped back there on Ellum Street," the man grumbled, "got me a bah-ul."

"Nothing in the house." My flesh felt like a cockroach nest.

"Sure there is, honeypie," Ethel told me. "That kye-auntie, compliments o Charlie."

"Wop wine, ain't it?" the man asked.

"Danged if I know," Ethel said.

"If it's wop," the man said, "don't bother. I eat American, drive American—"

"Bet you screw American," Ethel cut in.

"Used to wander everywhere, act like a A-rab," the man said. "Made me weary. Now I'm a settled-down Yank all the way. Only use brand-name stuff, to be sure."

"Don't you know," grinned Ethel, "that them wops buy wine from the U.S., then sell it back for profit?"

"That a fact?"

"Mamma, you know that chianti's fake," I said. "It never left this country."

"Naw, we'uns float it there from California in them oil tankers. Wops stick it in bottles, call it kye-auntie, and shoot it back return mail, he he."

He pondered this. "Guess I don't mind guzzling out of a wop bah-ul, if it's good old American wine inside."

Ethel nudged his ribs. "If it ain't goin in one end, it sure is comin out the other. Ain't that the trick Jesus turned?"

"Woman, don't badmouth Jesus," the man said. "Liable to call down trouble. The day of the Lord will come as a thief, in the which the heavens shall pass away with a great noise, and the elements shall be dissolved with fervent heat, and the earth and the works that are therein shall be burned up. Eleven Peter, three, nine."

"Eleven peter?" Ethel giggled. "Hear that, Amelia? One way or another, these men're gonna brag about their dang dicks. I'll run get the wine."

"That woman needs someone to supervise her mouth," the man said.

"Who the devil are you, Jasper?" I asked. "A refugee from the monastery?"

"Billy Graham." He gave me a snaggletoothed smile, so huge his brown tongue showed through the rotten spots and gluey strands of spit. "Alias I got for business. Only me and God knows my real name. Everybody else who knew is stone-dead." His grin opened like a grave, and he shuffled in his baggy, stained suit toward the couch. I scooted like Mercury and stuck the novel between us.

"Sleep in your clothes?" I asked.

"Don't hardly sleep," said Billy Graham, dropping his shapeless carcass beside me. A blast of rotten breath almost blinded me. "Too much memory on my mind. Wish I could drown it all. I been a thousand things in my life. Flew fighters in two wars. Caught tuna round Cuber—" His B.O. bridged the space between us, a fish-market stench, silver scales scattered over brick streets. "Once I hired out to that there Batista and in the dead of night done in a man sleeping behind gauze curtains. Cut him in half with a fillet knife. Then I turned fisher of men. Preached in tents all over Mexico and the Sou-western United States. Made and lost a fortune selling Jesus. It's how come they nickname me Billy Graham."

Ethel bounced in with the bottle and a butter knife. "Billy, tell her bout the goatfuck guy." She leaned down and whispered in my ear, "He's a damn liar like old Casey was."

"Worked," Billy went on, "picking guitar in the boo-dwar of old Ataturk, king of the A-rabs, while he put it to every one of God's creatures in his big high bed. Cats and little boys, small girls, chickens and dogs. Once his servant done brought him a sea lion knocked out with ether. But I lost that job when Ataturk finally croaked from the sif-lus he'd caught sticking his pole up a goat. Even so, he was the greatest king them A-rabs ever had."

Ethel plunked herself between us. Then she rammed the cork down the bottle neck with the knife, and wine splattered all over. "Billy," she said, "have a swig. Watch this here, Amelia."

When Billy swung the bottle to his yap, it was like the wine swished out into deep space. Not moving his throat, Billy sucked down half the bottle fast as the stuff dumped out, then wiped a cruddy sleeve across his lips and passed me what was left.

"How'd you manage that?" I was amazed.

"As a boy," Billy said, "I survived infantile paralysis, like Franklin Delano Roosevelt. For months, couldn't feel nothing, like a statue of stone. Then life seeped up my legs, into my butt. My balls come back to life. Life hit my chest, my shoulders and arms, my noggin. But it missed my neck. That's stone dead still. Stand me on my pate, what's in my belly drops out my mouth. Feels like I ain't really got a throat, but it's still there, and I got to take care of it. Food sticks in my craw and rots. So I got to spray in a powerful chemical to kill the stink. But I'm chug-a-lug champ of Arizoner and the Bahar Peninsular. Gimme a bah-ul, it's like flushing John Douglas." He thought a moment. "It's what drove me to crime, this throat. Yep, that's what done it."

I set the bottle in Ethel's lap. "Don't drink as a general rule. You two kill this."

"Was boxing champ of the Bahar, too," Billy Graham gargled. And I thought it would take a blowtorch at least to purify that throat of his. "Won m' crown killing this smart-mouthed longhaired faggot Mex in the ring. He went all over before the match saying I only had one ball, that he knowed, cause him and me'd done a trick in his hotel. Half into round two, I nailed that fruit farm up against a post and told him, 'Buddy, you done blowed your last greasy dick.' Split his skull open, dozen pieces. Brain sprayed in a gray cloud into row six. But it killed my career. Busted half the bones in both hands." Billy flexed those huge, gnarled claws, fingernails split and ragged, God knows what slime rotting underneath them. "Yeah, sweetchips, nowhere I ain't been, nothing I ain't done or seen. May of killed a man or two. But I sure brought a whole bunch more to life."

"Billy's father of our country, he he," Ethel said.

"Twelve times hitched," Billy bragged, "eighty-odd kids born in wedlock, plus three times more born out."

"How old are you, Jasper?" I asked. "A hundred fifty?"

"I'm your A-One bigamist," Billy Graham said. "Old Brigham Young don't hold a candle. Done waxed and multiplied, like the Lord wanted." He leered at me, eyeballs so mucky I couldn't tell where white flowed down the hole. "Lived with cannibals, too, and eat human flesh and drank human blood. My will says to freeze my corpse in a liquid nitrogen bah-ul, so when some smartass finds a cure for death, they can call me and my memories back. But it's mighty tiring for a man to do all there is. You need limits or you blow your steampipe. That's how come I'm American now to the bone, so I can live out my days in peace."

"Let's get down to business," Ethel said, "then hit the sack. Amelia, Billy thinks he can fence a few of them items upstairs."

"Show me where it's at, for, as Jesus said, where thy treasure is, there will they heart be also." Billy flushed the last wine down his dead neck, till the cork rested high and dry in the bottle's throat.

The front door opened. In walked Marlene holding hands with Jack Rader.

"Howdy, folks!" Jack said. "Marlene, this your granma and grampa?"

Marlene looked like she'd made a wrong turn heading for church and just come upon a barnyard orgy. Though her dress barely touched her crotch and she was turning red all over, up went that front of pure brass. "Grandpa Dollarhide drowned himself for some good reason," said Marlene. "Did they dredge him out of the oozy deep for our delight?"

"Cool it," I said.

"Children, name's Billy Graham." He unwound to a crooked-over six feet.

Marlene looked at Billy like he was a rat in the toilet. "Lord God, I can't take it," she sighed.

"Toljew that child needs a enema," Ethel said. "Or a powerful daddy roun the house to spank her cute ass."

"Any daddy of this little hunk," said Billy, "is gonna have a hard time minding his p's and q's. If any man thinketh that he behaveth himself unseemly toward his virgin daughter, if

86

she be past the flower of her age, and if need so requireth, let him do what he will, he sinneth not. Let them marry. One Corinthians, seven, thirty-six."

"More eleven peter." Ethel gouged an elbow into my breasts. "We'uns know old Casey'd of got a kick out o that."

"Whatever happened to your peach, Mamma?" I asked.

"Didn't know you hankered for fruits, Ethel, haw, haw," crowed Billy. Loose crud showered off him to my filthy floor.

"Jack, take me away from this." Marlene's voice quavered, small and low.

"Here's a fine young feller," Billy said. "Damn boys look like girls now. Ain't American. Doth not even nature itself teach you that, if a man have long hair, it is a dishonor to him?"

Ethel giggled. "That peter just keeps growin, don't it?"

"Haw haw haw," thundered Billy Graham.

Marlene stalked to where I sat. "How did that man crawl into my house? When is Grandma what's-her-name going to stop parking herself here? When is this mess going to end?"

I stood. And my scummy book flopped open on the couch. Marlene's keen eyes scanned the raunchiest passage in the X-rated thing, her lips making a disgusted pucker.

"That, uh, is for my college class," I said.

"I'm not staying in this house another night!" said Marlene.

"Doggone it, Marlene! What about your own filthy mouth? Sometimes I feel like tossing you into a sewer pipe and capping off both ends."

"I'm leaving," Marlene said.

"Where will you stay?"

"Jack'll find a place," Marlene said coolly. "Won't you, Jack?"

Jack Rader stood dangling his long arms, nervously tapping each finger of his right hand against his big toe.

"You're not shacking up with boys!" I shouted.

"If it weren't for my poor sisters, you wouldn't hear from me again." Saying that seemed to shock her. She bit her lip.

"I'll make you stay. I'll have the cops carry you back."

"Sure, Mamma. As if I don't know what's happening around here. That stuff in your room? Those noises last night? You're not calling the fuzz." Looking me hard in the eyes, she did something I wouldn't have expected—reached out, took my hands, said, "You're going to need help, Mamma. When you decide it's time, let me know." She turned to her bewildered hero. "Come on, Jack. We'll get my things later."

"Jack doesn't have a car!" I wailed.

"We're young and healthy. We can walk."

"Lord, if that's what you got in mind," Jack Rader said. "Mrs. Biggs, I sure as hell won't let her cause you too much grief." Marlene dragged him through the front door. "Don't worry, Mrs. Biggs. Your daughter's in good hands!" The door banged shut.

"So long, angelface," Ethel snorted. "C'mon, Billy. Might as well take Marlene's nice wide bed. Where does that grab you, Billyboy?"

"By jingo," croaked Billy Graham, "it grabs me by my middle limb. Hang a wop from this peach tree, you won't get no sway!"

Sewer gas can blow off the heaviest manhole cover. But try scooting that heavy lid back on. Till you do, no telling what squishy monsters will crawl out of the deep and cool your lap with slime.

CHAPTER *13*

Billy Graham was the Patron Saint of Thieves, and as such pocketed most of whatever he fenced as an Offering to his smelly self. But for all his stink, like fish bloated belly up in their tank, he fobbed off Charlie's junk for enough so we could limp along, the hottest items, he said, being the credit cards, and all those gold teeth, which bit right into the market's raging inflation. Billy dumped the Ithaca shotgun for a nice sum, he said, though of course kept the total amount secret from us. I kept the wee automatic in my nightstand to blast any crazy night visitor. The huge conch stayed as a doorstop in my bedroom. The LTD still gleamed at the curb with my battered Chevy. And $50,000 in phony bills gathered mung under my bed.

"What did Billy say about all those bogus hundreds?" I asked Ethel.

"Nothin," she said. "I'm keepin them back in case of dire need. Besides, we done goofed printin them so big. Got greedy. Bigger they are, harder they are to pass. But don't you fret. I'll put them to good use when the time is ripe. And only I know when that'll be."

Still, I was able to keep electricity and water, to hold back the bank from repossessing my home, and, most important, to pay half what I owed Gorgeous George and persuade him to unlock my credit once again. As for doctor, dentist, auto insurance, and Macy's, well, they could keep till I found another source of treasure—which I soon did after getting a letter signed, "Guess Who."

This time no censor had imposed a decent blackout on Superstud, the Hoosier Bluestreak. "Ho there, sweetheart," it said. "Ain't heard from the woman who is the most woman, so thought I would slip out this here by underground railroad, in case my last never made it past them shits upstairs. True to form, I been movin through this place like Ex Lax. In less time than a teenage boy gets his jollies I am a trustee working on cloud nine far from cornhole country. I am a servant in the mansion of His Royal Hindend, the Warden. Things is so slick, I ain't so anxious now to hack the world outside them gray walls.

"Some home comforts is hard to come by, which don't mean a man with brains and more than a ordinary amount of animal beauty can't get plenty. And the Warden sure is got a goodlooking strong wife.

"The two other servants is murderers, which is the most trustworthy crooks, but I can put on such a shine when there is a need to. When I land in this Holiday Inn, it hits me through the grapevine that the Warden is a fool for Jesus. So I start praying like a banshee, till my cellmate hollers, Won't you please ship this freak off to the convent? Next thing, I'm alone with the Warden in his office, lookin into his wet peepers, and we flop to our knees and beller Jesus! Jesus! All of a sudden the Warden throws hisself all over me like a dern fruitcake, blubberin that another lost soul is come to Glory. Which is how I come to serve him and his big hot wife.

"Me, the Warden and wife hit chapel together last Sunday. They give me a guitar and I done soloed Satisfied Mind, which ain't no hymn, but sure does pack some punch. By the time I finish warming them strings, that woman had her lap well watered, you could grow lilies in the bog, ha ha. Promised she'd slip out this here to a mailbox. Sure hate some pissant stranger sifting through my inmost thoughts.

"Back in the lonely slammer, my mind dwells on my wonderful ex, and I keep calling up mem'ries of old. Like when me and you got married that first time, and Bill Flank, who always hungered for your snatch, rounded up that batch of cut throats and trailed us to the Ron-Lee Motel. Before me and you could get down to business, the door busted open for a chivaree, which would of been a gangbang if I had not of still had on my shoes, and kicked them old boys ever which way. We had to move on to the Sundown Motel, clear over east of Goldengrove, across from the Police Lodge on that there little lake. We was mighty tired. But I bet the Sundown sold our mattress to a sideshow, she was so riddled with holes.

"How come you ever ditched me for that shit Errol, when you knowed it'd break my heart? Whether it's been through a carwash or inside a atom smasher, shit is shit is shit.

"Of course you say, if I loved to swing on your trapeze, how come after all those years I made that little detour with your old buddy Lillian Jones and wrecked our second go at marriage? Well, how come you needed that dang summer at the university when we was first married? Wasn't we doing great busting into them Naptown houses while fatcat owners soaked sun and grease in Florida? After another year, we would of retired free as kids. Then you got hots for your English teacher. When me and you got married again in Elm City, the East had done dried your sap. It was the straight and narrow, you said, which is dumb. No hill person wrote them laws, so they wasn't made for hill people to get by under. But try and tell some narrow minded judge.

"Well, what's past is dead and gone. And here I am in the Warden's home smack dab in the middle of offlimit goodies. But I do wish you was in super position ha ha to help out the old boy. It is one easy walk from the mansion to the free life, but how far does your jailbird fly without no money, or even no car? If I ain't out of here by Christmas time, my big wing will surely wither away."

Guess who wrote this filth. "That little detour with Lillian Jones" was a six-lane rainslick highway. On the sly, Lonzo paid her bus fare clear from Goldengrove to Elm City and set her up in a motel for one whole week, just to spite me. I don't greatly blame Lillian Jones, though. She was a good egg and in some ways a good high school friend years before.

But when it came to boys, she always did have the self-control of a lit firecracker, and Lonzo knew it. So it was his fault for taking advantage. By her sophomore year, Lillian Jones tooled through the track team, wrestling team, football team, the brass band, and Mr. Bill Combs, the art teacher everybody called a raving faggot, except Lillian Jones, who knew better. Twelve boys were having a beer blast and phoned her. "What sort of boys do you like, Lillian Jones?" they asked. "Boys with big peters," she replied. So half the hicks piled into a '49 Merc, picked her up at her shack, and went to work. By the time they touched open country, Lillian Jones was awash. One boy said, "Is she a mess." Another sang "Sloppy Seconds," to "Onward, Christian Soldiers." They stopped on the berm and opened the trunk, full of warm beer. A pair spread her legs, while somebody shook up a beer and foamed her clean. "What sort of boys you say you liked, Lillian Jones?" "All boys," Lillian Jones said, wearing only an innocent little smile. Then there was her closest high school buddy, Molly Fiddler, with the bow legs, who had even less self-control than Lillian Jones. Poor Molly wound up with me in reform school. But that's another story altogether.

After I blew my stack over Lonzo's letter, wanting to grab his thick sinewy neck and pull off his pinhead, I cooled down, realizing that he'd given me an inspiration. Why not raid the area around Errol's commune, those gorgeous empty summerhouses, and make off with whatever prizes fell into my lap? It was sinful, with people starving in shacks, for these mansions to stay hollow three fourths of the year. Of course, sooner or later they'd be torn down for some highway or highrise complex. Or the neighborhood would crumble, like mine, and some homes would become funeral parlors. And the red light would twinkle like Mars on the porch of others, and the swollen army of horny men would have yet more cathouses.

When Mr. Moon threw down his lopsided grin, I dressed for battle in black slacks and sweatshirt, and hid my blond hair in a black knit cap, then grabbed Ethel's gunnysack, and the flashlight off the icebox. I figured that in a posh neighborhood, Charlie's LTD was the ticket, not my battered Chevy.

Ethel saw me leaving. "You look like a dern commando. What's cookin?"

When I told her, she said, "Once you get set in motion, there's no puttin on your brakes, is there?"

"Only following your footsteps, Mamma. Come help."

"Naw, I'm too sick and creaky for such wild stuff. Just keep me posted on where you go and what you get. That'll give me kicks enough."

The night was like early spring, and few traffic lights slowed me, a pair of cautions that I ripped through. Then it was green all the way. I daydreamed like when I was a child, that I was a fighter pilot, blasting other drivers, shattering storefronts, riddling houses till boards and shingles flew every which way.

Though only a nail clipping, the moon flamed madly. So when I hit the road curving along the Sound, I could see which lawns were kept up and which were shameful messes. For the hell of it, I cruised past Errol's commune. Every light was burning, those snotty rich kids wasting juice like it was free. I triggered my machine guns and gave that pregnant beach house a broadside.

A mile further, I found just the target, a turreted doozy, gigantic and dark, the grounds such a shambles nobody could have touched them in years. Great weeds and beach grass thrust up. On the high porch, windblown sand had drifted like snow. It was more than I had hoped for my first night on the prowl, looming like a fake castle at the end of the world.

I drove past it, then doused my lights and turned up a side road with no houses, only brush, and huge trees dropping tons of shadow. Taking my flashlight and gunnysack, I headed across the wide beach to where waves smoothed the sand of prints. I could tell any deputy who might stop that I was digging clams, though they had long been poisoned by sewage.

A stone porch ate clear across the mansion's front, and

against the wall sand had drifted two feet deep. I found a window with its shutter busted. Somebody had poked a hole through the center pane, above the latch, and I wondered if maybe the Cat Burglar hadn't beaten me. But this place bore the stink of value, whereas the Cat Burglar specialized in getting nothing. And newspapers were more likely to find his poems down a shark's belly than here.

Careful not to slit my wrist on the jagged glass, I twisted the latch, then tugged the sash till it rose with a dusty groan. Open sesame. Heavy curtains coated me with dust. Inside, the thick damp smell recalled my shack on Pigeon Hill.

I snapped my flashlight on. Tangled over an oriental rug lay snake-size slugs, like Nature performed tricks in this dark hole she wouldn't dare in sunlight. Then I saw they were only fucking rubbers. Lowdown, ornery kids! What had gotten into young people, busting into a fine old home only to hold an orgy, then leaving slimy tracks all over? Mean nastiness! When I was a young girl, I wouldn't have done anything so rotten.

Wading carefully through the minefield of uglies, I shone my flashlight about the cavernous room. Some master, it seemed, had carved delicate shapes in the rich wood lining walls and ceilings—grapes, apples, birds singing among tangled leaves, knotted grass, vines circling sapling trunks, sweet faces of children peeking through rosebushes, a wooden sun in a wooden sky. What looked like an organ covered one end of the room, floor-to-ceiling gold pipes, keyboard an old-fashioned crescent doohickey with two wide pedals. Overstuffed chairs and couches squatted everywhere, probably all some famous brand name. The room seemed so rich and lovely I felt I'd walked into a cathedral.

Amelia, I thought, you're here on business. So I moved into a long hallway, covered floor to ceiling on both sides with maybe twenty thousand books, mildewed and swarming with silverfish. I pulled a few off the shelf and saw they had been inscribed. "For Louis. Here's looking forward to the Sun King's next anthology. Ernest." "This copy to dear

Louis, to the memory of outlandish hospitality. Willa." And then I found one that really shocked me, a copy of the filthy novel I'd read for night class, signed by its author. "Stick this in your next compendium. Henry." Why, I wondered, would a cultured man like Louis allow such trash in his house, too?

But what could I take with me? The longer I stayed, the harder it grew to even think about business. On I walked, exploring, and reached a vast glass sun porch, with not one pane busted. There sat a long wood table, six wood chairs pushed back as if a family had just risen from breakfast on those plates, food stains underneath the dust. On the table lay a yellowed Sunday paper, November, 1963.

Its front page knocked *my* windows out, because it showed President Kennedy, whose funeral was to be that day, and his wife and little daughter. Sifting through the crackly pages, I saw that photo of Kennedy in swimtrunks, some gal in a bikini looking like she'd love to jump him on the spot. Well, my feelings of eight years back flooded in, because John Kennedy could have put this shoes under my bed anytime. But Kennedy's eyes did sit too close together, and Camelot was genuine plaster of Paris, and he was rumored to have the morals of certain other great statesman studs like randy old Ben Franklin and Aaron Burr.

One article reminded me that Kennedy had saved a wounded man's life, swimming him to shore when Kennedy himself was badly wounded. In the fiery circle my flashlight tossed, I saw my tears falling. Really look up to somebody, and you're bound to get screwed in the end.

So I moved on. And right off the bat, I found plunder. In the kitchen big enough for the Waldorf, I dumped a tray of sterling silver jangling into Ethel's bag. Upstairs in a carved dresser, spiderwebs spanning its mirror, I found brooches and delicate pins, a class ring, and a square gold medal with Greek letters.

Then I gingerly spelunked a basement that dripped with slimy ooze. The foundation was fieldstone, the floor mostly dirt, An octopuslike furnace sent pipes in all directions, and off in one corner sat a huge deepfreeze. I heard its thick hum above the crickets. After all these years, A.C. still goosed the house.

Out of curiosity, I lifted the top, half expecting a body, but finding only a heap of frosted packages, clearly meat. I leaned in. But what if I fell and the top dropped? All I could hope for then was that those vandals might come back right away and find me.

Moving away, I came to a small iron grate in the basement wall, which led to a dank room. Lining its four walls were wine racks with room for enough bah-uls to stock Billy Graham's heaven. But mostly they held huge, gorgeous spiderwebs, like clouds. Looking at the most splendid web, its maker a dusty hunk, I wondered what accident lets spiders spin a thing so orderly and beautiful, when they don't know beans about beauty and destroy the creatures they snag.

I pulled out the only four bottles that remained, mouldy and damp, Château Something-or-other, 1937, a brand name I didn't know and couldn't pronounce. This is a place you can visit again, I thought, and lounge around like a child's dream playhouse. I took the bottles with me, unaware that the house's real treasure was its wine. Heading for the steps, I tripped over a cord. The freezer stopped its hum.

Upstairs a weird idea came to me. I tore loose the endleaf from Henry's filthy book, then searched till I dug a pencil stub out of an overstuffed chair. I printed:

> I specially love to break in houses
> Of wealthy fatcats, spoiled louses.
> Seems to me its mighty fitten
> For this poor chilly little kitten

At which point, I got stuck. Finally I made do with:

> To trade in your doojies on a hot wool mitten.

I liked how it began, but not how it finished, rhymes scrapping with sense. A kitten would need four mittens, if any. And I held a much higher opinion of Louis. But my flashlight batteries were almost dead. Maybe I could rewrite the next time I came back. I signed myself "Cat Burglar" and laid the poem among the rubbers. Then I kissed my Cracker Jack ring for luck, dropped my booty through the window I'd entered by, and stepped gingerly out.

Lord, it was a lovely walk back. The monster under that huge black mass of water lay relaxed. Elm City cast a great halo into the sky. The moon drew fire onto the water, and I saw burning pinpricks of windows across the Sound. Beauty opened me out. I remembered other nights I'd spent by water, a clambake during happier times, Marlene and Jenny small children making sand castles, while Joy, Michael, Errol, and I buried a thirty-gallon whiskey barrel upright, leaving its lip in the air, then dove for seaweed. We heated stones between fuming layers of charcoal, till at last broad-backed Michael shoveled white-hot stones into the barrel. We dumped in sea water. Steam roared from hell. We followed fast with armloads of seaweed. A dozen lobsters clicked to white-eyed death, seaweed, a bushel of live clams, seaweed, corn, potatoes. We lashed the tarp to the barrel's steaming mouth, piled a mound of sand over it, then boozed, hollered, and swam till we threw open the treasure chest savory with cooked flesh, and feasted like kings.

I thought of times still more strange, the sweet water of the L-shaped limestone quarry near my childhood shack on Pigeon Hill, the terrifyingly deep quarry they took the Empire State Building out of. My daddy brought me swimming there on hot days, though a hundred swimmers had drowned in those depths. I clung to his slippery back while he streaked like a dolphin, his poor hands and feet scarcely more than flippers from war wounds and the bite of a moray eel. Remembering, I felt the surface of my heart pop open. And I was thinking of nothing. My heart gulped in Long Island Sound, and I was beach, water, full of filth and sewage, sky, stars, city's smoky halo, flying, winning the only Grand Prize.

I landed breathless, holding a gunnysack, a dead flashlight, wondering where I'd parked my car.

97

CHAPTER *14*

It was a crazy fall. The leaves died as usual, and turned beautiful. But a sunny day would feel like summer coming back, and my blood would warm up a summer mood, like the night I first started raiding the summer homes of the rich and idle. Then suddenly it would grow so cold I expected to see birds frozen inside a sky of solid ice, and breaking into one of those houses, around midnight, was entering an igloo. If the season didn't always make sense, I could still count on the moon, moving through her phases cool and serene. The moon was at the end of its first quarter one Saturday in November, when Jenny turned thirteen, two days after getting her first period.

When the flow had hit Marlene, she was only eleven, and it was enough to break my heart. First Marlene refused one morning to climb out of bed. Next thing I knew, she'd been in the bathroom three hours, leaving only when I promised to go downstairs. Then she rushed back into her room, where she stayed all day without eating. I woke at midnight to hear her sobbing, and this time when I knocked she let me in, then zipped back under the covers. "Mamma," she said, "I'm dying."

"What on earth?"

"I'm bleeding to death, Mamma." And she told me the section of pasture it came from.

"Oh, honey, it's the most natural thing in the world."

But I felt guilty enough to die for never having warned her, assuming, I guess, that in the disaster area of my life, she'd absorb the knowledge by osmosis.

When Jenny's time came, though, she already knew the curse and its tracks. At six of an icy morning, she knocked on my bedroom door and asked, "Mother, is there any Kotex in the house?" If Marlene had been with us, Jenny would have gone to her with her wound, but Marlene was living in Jack Rader's apartment, and I felt helpless to do a thing about her. I was surprised Jenny didn't wake up Ethel, because those two had grown mighty close, with Ethel trimming Jenny's fat off. "Don't touch that there bun," she'd say. "Eat the cottage cheese and the beansie-weensies. You can gobble them things till they're comin out your butt an not gain a ounce."

"Ethel, how come you don't follow your own advice?" I'd asked.

"Dirty Billy wants soft chunks to grab. But it ain't natural for a child to be a fatso."

"Yes, Grandmother," Jenny would say, delicately pronging some baked beans. "If that's your advice."

"You're not stuffing enemas into her like you did me, with God knows what evil ends in mind."

"Why, this here's a house of virtue," Ethel leered. "Pope's gonna license it a convent, make us gals all traipse round in black puptents."

On the morning of Jenny's birthday, I staggered down in my blue robe to stifle a pounding on my door, plus a sound like a garbage disposal chewing raw bone.

Joy Silverspring, blowing smoke from her nostrils, stood there with Michael, who I hadn't seen for months. Usually, Michael looked sulky, like his organs itched deep inside where he couldn't scratch. But now, carrying a book and a white bundle, he was beaming like the devil had devoured his worst enemy. All the racket roared out of this bundle.

"How're you doing, Michael?" I asked.

"GRRRRREAT!" he hollered. "YOU WOULDN'T BELIEVE HOW GREAT!"

"Glad to hear it," I said.

Joy Silverspring didn't look great. "Hello, Amelia." She stepped in. "Michael, Amelia might as well see the source of that roar."

Michael peeled back the wrapper on what looked like a plastic bag of oleo in the early fifties, lard-white till you popped a seal and kneaded the gunk orange. But margarine, unlike a roasting saint, was quiet.

"Why, it's a little baby," I finally said. "What's its name, Joy?"

"Axel," Joy announced in a flat voice. "Michael picked the world's ugliest name."

"It's a *great* name!" Michael beamed. "The little fellow sure has us going in circles."

"Ha ha," Joy said. "Tell Amelia how you found God, Michael."

"It was late one night," Michael said, shifting the fifteen pounds of squawling oleo into my arms, where it bucked like a headless chicken. "I was driving back from Rye."

Bess came whirling in from the kitchen, scattering crayons in all directions. "What's making the noise, Mommy?" Since Ethel arrived and Marlene left, Bess, who never belonged in the Peaceable Kingdom anyway, had been acting like that Tasmanian Devil in Bugs Bunny.

"Baby Axel," I said.

"I want to smell it!" Bess shouted over Axel's ruckus. "Hum. A big poopie!" She whirled away.

"Wonderful," said Joy. "Got a few pointers on child-raising, Amelia?"

"I was flying along in the Mercury," Michael went on, dead to interruptions, "after a prayer-meeting with Dr. Wierwoo—"

"Who?" I asked.

"Weirdo," Joy said.

"—all I had was a Gulf card and three dollars cash." Michael settled his wide rear on a bundle of newspapers. "And my gas gauge said empty. I passed Texaco, Shell, but no Gulf where I could use the credit card." He dug into his short wiry hair and raked his scalp. Joy once told me Michael's fur was so thick and steelwooly it stalled out electric clippers. Michael also had a thick loam of dandruff that nothing cleaned except those cats, who'd heap around his scalp when he lay down, and purr till they'd licked the last loose scale. White silt now seeped over both Michael's big ears.

"Finally, I gave up," he was saying. "I pulled into a BP and bought three dollars' worth of regular."

As Axel writhed in my arms like a case of bubonic plague, Michael uncorked the Bible from his armpit and flipped it open. "Therefore take no thought," he read loudly above Axel's furious shrieks, "saying, what shall we eat? or, what shall we drink? or, wherewithal shall we be clothed? for your heavenly Father knoweth that ye have need of all these things. But seek ye first the kingdom of God, and his right-eousness, and all these things shall be added unto you."

"That there my buddy eleven peter?" Ethel shouted down the stairs.

"Eleven what?" asked Michael.

"Ethel, come meet some folks."

"Somebody can't read roman numerals," Michael said. "She must mean Two Peter."

Wearing a ratty blue robe, Ethel threaded around rags, string balls, and a skillet with a hole through its middle. "Two peter? That's a wrinkled shame!"

"Anyway, I drove around the next curve," Michael said, "and found my Gulf station. If I'd had faith in Father, He would have succored my needs. I could have filled my tank and arrived home with cash in my pocket."

"Pure accident," I said, scarcely able to believe what I'd just heard.

"Accident?" Michael looked at me like he'd never known of such a thing.

"Coincidence," I said.

"But that's Father showing his hand." Michael lit up like he'd stumbled over the most brilliant mare's nest ever. "Coincidence is Divinity," he announced. "Accident is Father's Signature."

"His signature," sniffed Joy. "Ha. Another damned brand

name like Gulf or Zenith, and just as meaningful." She stuffed a fag between her lips and lit it from a smoking butt. "Wish Father would change diapers and wipe hindends."

"That there ever shut off?" Ethel asked.

"Its father called hogs," Joy said.

Michael flipped wildly through his Bible. "Suffer little children to come unto me," he read, "and forbid them not: for of such is the kingdom of God." He paused. "And whoso shall receive one such little child in my name receiveth me."

"Rather receive eleven peter, he he," Ethel sniggered.

While Axel swiveled the dead in their vaults, I recalled that my oddball teacher had raved recently about Jesus. Some critic, he'd told us, wrote that the hero of my filthy Paris novel was a Christ figure. "S-s-so? Then what about the Stigmata Kid? He's got to be some kind of Figure too, right? A Captain Midnight Figure, Joe Palooka Figure, or Jolly Green Giant Figure, so he'll *mean* something! My God, it's worse than a schizophrenic who mistakes a total stranger for his long lost father and kills the poor bugger. Or a paranoid who thinks he's Napoleon." I'd have to get his comments on Michael's discovery.

"We oughta be able to find this noisy little thing a present upstairs," Ethel said. "C'mon, Amelia."

I returned Axel to Joy.

"And I need to use your john," Michael said.

Upstairs, I knocked on Jenny's door. "Wake up, honey. Happy birthday." Jenny's springs creaked, and I wondered if Errol Shiflet would remember what day this was. I hadn't remembered myself, till the night before, too late to get her a present.

Twelve feet off, Michael peed noisily.

"I was awakened, Mother," Jenny said, "by the music of the spheres." She had taken over first violin in the wiseacre section from Marlene. She had also lost twenty pounds, and wore a smile both peaceful and saintly.

I just finished dressing, when Ethel barged into my room. "What we gonna give that little Axel?"

Rummaging under my bed in the dregs of what had come

from Ethel's gunnysack, I pulled out the rabbit's foot. "This'll do," I said. "But more important, what is there for Jenny's birthday?"

"I vote for them Trojans," Ethel leered.

Digging further, I found the Timex pocket watch. "This is all I have. I've come to a poor pass, almost forgetting my child's birthday."

"It's a brand name, if that's any comfort," Ethel said.

In the john, the toilet seat was awash. Michael might have gone religious, but his brain was still 100 per cent pure dog. Maybe Father would collar him in a heaven with toilet seats in every cloud, where Michael could pee up a storm.

Downstairs in the kitchen, accompanied by Axel's caterwauling, Bess was whipping off a masterpiece in red and blue crayon.

"What's that?" Michael asked her. It looked like a tornado of scribbles.

"The little boy stole the baby kittens," Bess said. "The police was very vornated."

"Very what?" asked Joy.

"Vornated!" Bess shouted, narrowing her eyes and taking off to another part of the house.

"Vornated," Michael said. "Angry, frustrated, bewildered. Excellent word, vornated. I'll use it in a poem." He wandered absently into the dining room.

Aim carefully, I thought, next time you vornate into my john.

Axel blew his trumpet in Joy's arms, while Ethel dangled the rabbit's foot in his face."

"Gag him with it," Joy shouted, "before I vornate myself!"

"You aren't used to babies," I told her. "At first they're all commotion and poop, but later they're a pleasure."

"I heard Marlene ran off with some man," Joy came back.

Why did I put up with this woman? Well, I had to pity someone married to Michael Silverspring. And when I groaned through two of my divorces, Joy did tender her hot, bony shoulder to cry on.

"I raised Marlene to be tough and independent," I said. "If Marlene stood naked in a snowstorm, she'd survive."

"I know just how she'd do it, too." Joy gritted her teeth like she was about to bite through Axel's neck.

"I'm calling up Billy Graham," Ethel said. "He'd love to jaw with someone else that knows the Good Book so well. If we'uns is gonna have us a party, you need to lay in some stores." She was stuffing the rabbit's foot into her robe, when Joy suddenly grabbed it and wound the chain round her finger.

"Do that," Joy said. "Take Michael along, will you, and this Axel? Michael, haul your ass in here."

"Coming, darling." Though Michael was made of mungballs and crumbly erasers, he had a springy, graceful walk, like Ethel, who'd scattered the rest of her goods all over Indiana in operating rooms.

Joy dumped Axel into Michael's arms. "That child could be the most effective birth-control apparatus uncovered by man," she said. "One look, and any sane woman would stitch herself shut."

Walking to Gorgeous George's, I asked Michael, "What's happened to you and Joy?"

"Joy won't accept Father," Michael said. "But it's just as well. As Father said, so because thou art lukewarm, and neither hot nor cold, I will spew thee out of my mouth."

Little Axel blew twenty cubic yards of gas from his hindend.

"Amen," I muttered.

"Your mother's quite a lady," Michael said. "Does she have religion?"

"Only eleven peter."

"If you accept Jesus," Michael said, "He enters that part of the body, too."

"Michael, did Jesus say whether the world was round or flat?" I asked.

"He wasn't concerned with science," Michael answered. "Only the soul. Matter could go its wicked, disorderly way."

104

"Didn't Jesus say someplace that thinking bad was as big a sin as doing bad?"

"Hold Axel, will you?" Michael animated his Bible, and read, "Ye have heard that it was said by them of old time, Thou shalt not commit adultery: But I say unto you, That whosoever looketh on a woman to lust after her hath committed adultery with her already in his heart."

"Then why isn't just thinking *good* as virtuous as going out and actually doing good?"

"What?" said Michael.

"Another thing. You said Jesus enters into eleven peter."

"If you accept Him," Michael said.

"But you also said, as far as Jesus was concerned, the world of matter could just go its wicked way. Eleven peter is surely matter."

"Oh," Michael said.

"So you make no sense whatever."

"God, Amelia." He kicked the sidewalk. "Lay off, will you? Joy nags me all day, except when she's out God knows where, or I'm at the library. She smokes like a chimney, filthy habit. It's enough to make me do something desperate. And as for logic," he cried, "I've had it up to here! I write poems, those ingrown academic toenails, because I've got to publish to keep my job, and Joy won't cook anymore and Axel lies around all day in a dirty diaper, and when I come home late from the library, Joy's gone and Axel's raising Cain, and the only part of the house she keeps straight is the top of her goddamn dresser!"

And she stopped wiping your bottom, I thought, and your pee off the john.

"There are experiences beyond logic," he said, "that make you feel at one with the universe."

"Michael, have you ever had one?"

After a long pause, he said, "I don't know. But with everything in the world upside down, we need something to hang on to, don't we?"

The overhead bell tinkled as we entered Champion's.

"Mrs. Shiflet-Biggs!" George thundered from behind the meat. "And Mr. Silverspring, whom we have not seen for ages. How are you, sir?"

A switch clicked in Michael's spine. "Just simply *grrreat!*" he cried.

Mrs. Champion peeked out from behind the cash register and chimed, "Oh, look there at that sweet child. Oh, George, it's a tiny baby." Bustling wee and round into the main part of the small store, she stuck out her arms for the squawling packet.

"Oh, the sweetheart," she cooed. Uncovering Axel's clenched face, which roared with spit, she kissed his forehead tenderly. "The darling wonder." Axel sucked in a giant breath. I stuck both fingers in my ears, expecting balloons to blow at both the child's ends. But no noise came.

"Oh, lovely thing," Mrs. Champion whispered.

"Ah, goooo," Axel said.

"Perfect little baby."

"Gurrrrk-uuh," said Axel.

"Woman! Now, woman!" Giant George's yap hung open, shrill terror filled his eyes.

Nestling warm and snug against Mrs. Champion's huge, pillowy bosom, Axel now looked like a small human being, not at all like a sack of oleo.

"He needs changing," sighed Mrs. Champion. Holding Axel steady as a ship's compass, she scurried to the disposable diapers, expertly tore a box open, plucked a Pamper, spread Axel tenderly beside the cash register, and went to work on him.

"Oh, woman," moaned George, without one iota of pep.

"Nice store, George," Michael said.

"If it's so nice," scowled George, "why don't you shop it more? And you"—scowling at me—"when do you plan to settle the rest of your account?"

"Ahhh-brrrrrg," Axel said.

"Hand me the distilled water, Mr. Silverspring," Mrs. Champion said. "And some baby oil, above the diapers. And a box of Kleenex."

"Baby oil, woman?" gasped Mr. Champion. "Distilled water? Kleenex! Ah! Oh!"

"It's okay, George," I said. "While your wife's anointing Axel, I'm going to charge us a birthday party."

When we got outside, the chilly day cooled Mrs. Champion's love, and Axel, in Michael's thick arms, proceeded to raise the dead. "My spirits need lifting," Michael said. "Think you could afford some booze?"

"I'm afraid to prime Joy anymore than she is already, for fear she'll go hog-wild."

"Who's around to go hog-wild with?" Michael asked. "Let's stop here at Bill-Mar."

"Jesus won't mind," I said. "He turned out homemade."

The booze cost me a bothersome $25. I had $125 cash on me, left over from the $300 Billy gave us after he'd fenced my Treasure House takings. Lord knows crime wasn't making us rich, and I'd begged Ethel to doctor a few ones to look like twenties, or at least go out and hang enough paper to see us through the month. But she kept insisting she was "retired from active duty." "Just keep me posted on what you're up to," she said, "and I'll supervise." As for that fortune in bogus hundreds, she wouldn't hear yet of putting it to work. "Time ain't ripe, sweetie pie, and that's all there is to it."

Lugging Axel and Gideon, Michael was no help with the sacks, so I was glad to reach home.

"Isn't that Errol's car?" Michael asked. "The black, smashed-up, ugly little pile of junk?"

"He remembered Jenny's birthday after all."

Errol met us at the door. "Michael, you crazy bastard!" He slapped Michael's back. "How's that diploma mill where I busted my ass?"

"Grrreat!" Michael said. But his eyes looked terrible.

"Hear you finally got a son and heir," said Errol.

"You're hearing it all right," Michael replied.

Errol relieved me of a sack. "Christ, look at the booze! Where'd you shoplift this?"

The door shut behind me. I stumbled into a den of thieves.

"Amelia shoplifted?" Joy asked, smiling at me over Errol's shoulder.

"Hey there, sweetchips!" croaked Billy Graham from the living room. "Got another bah-ul for old Billy? Where's the Bible-spouter?"

"Amelia does have lots of money all of a sudden," Joy said.

"Because I stumbled onto a treasure," I told her.

"Mommy," Bess called, "Jenny won't let me show my bottom!"

"Marlene shown up?" I asked.

"Marlene's too wore out with wickedness to care," Ethel said.

"Hello, Mother." Jenny stood amidst the trash. She wore a skirt of Marlene's, which let most of her hang out, and I thought Michael Silverspring was going to crack his eyeballs staring.

"Ummy-yum." Errol waved a half gallon of Old Crow in one hand, a half gallon of Cutty Sark in the other. "Let's fuck up our brains."

"Watch your tongue, Jasper," I said.

"Are you really off on a criminal rampage, honey?" Joy asked me.

"Whaaaaaggh!" roared Axel.

Errol Shiflet, Ph.D., tumblerful of hooch in hand, whacked Jenny's rump. "Ethel, you're another Pygmalion."

"Igpay Atinlay?" Ethel asked.

"Speak American," said Billy Graham, peering through a wet glass. "I just heaved down a half bah-ul of foreign shit."

"Know what I've always thought about a woman with full-grown children?" Michael whispered in my ear. "That she'd be stretched loose as a cow. Isn't true, though, is it, Amelia?" He handed me a glass and licked his thick lips.

"Go slobber into your damn Bible, Michael."

As Michael stumbled toward Billy on the couch, one of his ten-pound hands brushed my bottom. The man on the flying trapeze began a double flip down in my guts and I drowned him with bourbon.

"Thought you shunned demon rum." Errol pounded me between the shoulder blades.

"Sweet Jesus, it hurts!" Ethel cried. Balled up at Billy's feet, knees touching her chin, she pawed her belly.

"Shouldn't of chug-a-lugged," Billy said. Beside him, Michael mumbled into his Bible.

"Feel better?" Errol asked me.

"Don't touch me with your clap," I coughed out. "Don't touch Jenny, either."

"Ethel said you wanted to meet my old man," Errol whispered, "to do a job on the foul cutthroat."

"Errr-ol," Joy crooned, halfway down the stairs.

"What were you doing up there?" I asked.

"Sniffing your bicycle seat, darling," Joy said. "Come along, Errol."

My glass brimmed with booze. Then it was empty. Jenny sat beside Billy in Michael's lap, and Michael read, "There is therefore now no condemnation to them that are in Christ Jesus." He flipped pages. "Now this. Where sin abounded, grace did abound more exceedingly. Add those up, Billy."

"I git the gist," Billy croaked.

"Once Father has chosen you for his team, you can't sin," Michael said. "Lord, my bladder is bursting."

"Krrraaaaghunk!" writhed Axel, a lump on the dining-room floor.

"Jesus, this here's tasty." Billy lowered a bottle from his dead throat. And I saw he had found the Château Something-or-other, 1937. "It's the real stuff, all righty."

"It's been caged up too long," Joy whispered against my ear. "Like steam in a pressure cooker." Hair mussed, lipstick melted like butter, her face mooned all hot and bright into mine. "Darling, Michael is hot to trot after Jenny. Do you feel left out? Do you want somebody, too?"

"I feel so strange," I said.

"Child, it's because you're so wild!" Joy gave me a big sudden hug, scrunching me with her skeleton. She trembled so violently, I knew that if she ever popped her cork, Michael had himself a volcanic bedful. "Honey." Her lips scalded my ear. "Remember saying what a mess of fun it is to go bust?"

"Hold me up like that, Joy. It feels good."

"You were right," Joy whispered, and planted a wet kiss on my neck. "I never knew so much pleasure was just lying around."

"Is Michael shooting out of the same cannon as yours?"

"I've got my own powder charge," Joy said. "I'm not even thinking about a net to catch me when I land!"

On the floor in front of the fireplace, I hugged a stack of newspapers.

"Mamma, please! What are you doing?"

"Marlene, honey?"

"Oh, Mamma, let me help you up," begged Marlene.

"How come you went and left me? How many women and children did Jack dump for that medal?"

"You're flying drunk, Mamma, and this place has gone mad. I found Bess in the kitchen playing with sharp knives. Grandma's in the bathroom sick as a dog. Michael Silverspring is pawing Jenny. And there's a baby under the dining-room table with St. Vitus' dance."

"You left your mamma for a big toe."

"You're impossible!" Marlene wailed.

A warm, sweaty animal held me while I swam in the quarryhole, in the murky green. "I've loved you for thirteen years, Amelia." I slit my lids open. Michael Silverspring was hugging me on the floor. "Where are you, really, Amelia? Where do you center? Do you hate all men?"

A fish churned inside my stomach. I pounded the bathroom door till it opened. "Lemme die peaceful," Ethel whined. But I pitched her off John Douglas, then gripped the seat and fired squid and Red Devils and God knows what crud into the deep.

CHAPTER *15*

The day after Jenny's birthday, I was vornated in one end and out the other, and so was Ethel. My tummy worked like an Electrolux, tube stuck in its back end to blow out trapped hunks of mung. Every half hour, I bounced into the john, retched and dry-heaved and death-rattled like a jalopy with steam dynamiting the radiator. Finally, I sent Jenny out for a king-size bottle of Pepto-Bismol, which helped. But the next morning, there I was tossing my cookies all over again. Kid, I thought, if I didn't know better, I'd think you had a case of morning sickness. Ha ha—

Back I counted on fingers and toes to that night before Ethel came, ran out of digits, started over. Lord God, that damned screwball!

At once I phoned Dr. Burke's secretary, whose voice was like a chain saw, for an emergency appointment.

"Mamma," I called through Marlene's door, "what can I tell Dr. Burke about you?"

"Can he resurrect the dead?" Ethel groaned.

"You're just hung over, Mamma."

"After two days? Honey, tuck me in pine an pay the undertaker cold cash."

Dr. Burke's office was a wilting yellow house in a cruddy armpit of Elm City. In my neighborhood, people still occupied most houses, but in Dr. Burke's most were condemned, the people run out. When the steel ball crushed those houses, a tidal wave of rats was expected to overwhelm the rest of us.

His waiting room, walls dead-skin yellow, was crammed with women, newborns blowing noise and snot, unborns still in the oven. Since Dr. Burke was a randy goat, he no doubt relished each poor shapeless creature as a treat, once he dragged her onto the table and yanked her drawers off. A small, wide man of fifty, he also did everything with a cigar oozing between his lips. His six wives divorced him. Who could stand a downpour of ashes whenever the doctor's plumbing flushed? But he was a good sort and charged little, poor man, knowing his true market value.

"What is it, Mrs. Biggs?" he asked, voice high-pitched, nervous. Stogie fuming in his jaw, he sat on the table's metal top, fat thighs swinging over the side, feet a yard off the floor.

"Got myself pregnant," I said.

"Parthenogenesis?" Dr. Burke talked like a dictionary.

"What?"

"Virgin birth," he said, dropping off the table like Humpty Dumpty. "Let's take a gander at your problem." And suddenly Dr. Burke hoisted me onto the table, ripped off half my clothes, pried my legs apart and plunged in a junk-yard of cold steel.

"Lord God, that *hurts!*" I cried, as if my privates were an unhealed wound.

"Lots of women out there waiting to see this medic. Rush rush rush," he mumbled around his weed.

"You're *hurting!*" I felt steel halfway to my heart.

"Yessir. Want to have this child, Mrs. Biggs? Right now, it's a spider egg. In a few weeks, it'll be a fish, then a cat. Evolution is taking place in your belly. But all you have this morning is protozoa." I felt breath against my bottom. Smoke rose.

Suddenly I remembered why this man, who sounded like he had brains, was stuck in the world's butt, drank like a fish, his life ripped to scrap.

"Operation's a breeze," he was saying.

Years ago, a young intern, Dr. Burke had performed his maiden tonsillectomy. His foot slipped on the operating-room floor, his whole body dropped one terrible inch, and he sliced an artery in a little girl's throat. Sleeping, she died in a fountain of blood.

"No," I said.

"I could peel off twenty a day."

"Not on your life."

His mug rose unhappily over my belly, like a diver coming up for air. "You don't want to be aborted? Or you don't want me— Don't answer that one."

"Hey, look, nothing personal."

"I'm probably the smartest man you'll ever meet. I was a superb student. I could have made history." His voice died in a sigh. He walked to his desk and made a phone call, speaking low so I couldn't hear. Hanging up, he said, "Get dressed. Here's a place at Elm City University." While he scribbled on a prescription pad, I started pulling on my clothes. Scattered between my legs on the shiny table were specks of dried gore, sprayed there while he was gouging like a gravedigger. Then I saw they were drippings off his fat cigar.

"Med School classmate of mine heads the O.B. section," he said. "Looks like a quarterback. You'll love him. Here, hand this to the lady at the door. Your ticket to the world of success, where nobody makes a small human slip-up and wrecks his whole life. Always a pleasure to see you, Mrs. Biggs."

I drove ten miles, through most of the city, to the Med School, where a pair of huge red-brick smokestacks poured tons of junk into the blue sky. At their base lay this gray jerry-built hovel, which reminded me of the grisly reform school I'd been cooped in during my teens, flight barracks of an ancient airfield with weed-split runways. One day a week they let us take a two-minute shower in a foul-smelling hutch, under a matron's steely eyes. I parked my LTD between the smokestacks and entered the building.

Wooden chairs, maybe a hundred, lined both sides of a long hall packed with girls, most no older than Marlene, and some younger than Jenny. At the hallway's end, a pair of swinging doors swallowed one child after another.

I handed a pleasant-looking lady my ticket. "Mrs. Biggs?

We'll try to take you soon." My advanced age, no doubt. "Please complete this." She gave me a clipboard, ballpoint chained to it. The form asked rude questions like, "Who is responsible for your condition? Husband. Fiance. Boy friend. Other." Where it said "Religion," I circled "None." It even asked the types of contraceptive I'd used during my life. "One type too few," I wrote.

A child insisted creaky, feeble me take her chair. "Thanks, dear." Three teen-agers to my right, in tight blue jeans, T-shirts, no bras, had billfolds open in their weeny laps to look at pictures.

"Isn't he groovy?"

"Super!"

"Like, you know, my boyfriend he—" pointing to a snapshot of some greaseball in a white dinner jacket.

Suddenly the children were showing me their pictures. "Why, that sure is a handsome youngster," I said. "And him, too. He looks just like—"

"Tab who?"

One of those movie stars Errol insisted was a roaring faggot.

And then I thought of the reform school surgeon, and the evil wing-clipping he gave poor Molly Fiddler.

My turn came to enter a cubbyhole office. A wise old gal leaned clear across her desk where the form I'd filled out lay, and shook my hand as if I'd earned the Purple Heart. "Very pleased, Mrs. Biggs. Most people don't hang on to their sense of humor in here. I'm Susan Smith."

I settled into an easy chair.

"Dr. Carter will examine you," she said. "We'll put you in University Hospital, and you'll be out for dinner. Procedure takes fifteen minutes."

"Is procedure the same as abortion?" I asked.

"Abortion?" She told how the doctor would shoot me with dope to numb my womb, burrow in a tube stuck to something like a vacuum cleaner, and suck out—"tissue," she called it.

"I call them babies," I said.

114

She looked kind and motherly, as she said, "Frankly, we don't want you as a psychiatric basket case. Tell me, Mrs. Biggs, any reservations about the procedure?"

"No. I don't know."

"Ever undergone this procedure before?"

I felt trembly. "When I was a little girl, I . . . miscarried."

"Who was the father?" Sharp, quick.

"Don't know."

The wise old eyeballs drilled me. "And this one?"

"Don't even want to know," I said.

"Afraid who it might be?"

"What do you mean?" I couldn't stop trembling.

"You tell me what I mean."

I took a breath and hung tight to the chair. "That ah the daddy might be colored?"

Her look softened. "Is that really it?"

"Yes!" I rubbed my green ring for luck, and some old song fluted through my mind for no reason, "His brain was so loaded it nearly exploded." I wished Marlene could armor me with her brass, because suddenly I was trying to remember something very important but couldn't. It was like part of me inside had gone dead—still there, but I couldn't feel it anymore.

"All right, Mrs. Biggs. Now I'll send you to Dr. Carter." Rising, she reached for my hand. "It's been"—her eyes were shocking, so bright and clear, like X rays—"interesting."

I flew out into the hall and let the swinging doors gulp me. Dr. Carter was a broad-shouldered, blond, blue-eyed man with a killing smile. "Hello, Mrs. Biggs." He burrowed his huge hands into the rubber, then helped noose my legs gently into the stirrups. "You're in good shape, so the procedure should be uneventful. They'll tell you where to go. Next."

Where to go was the main hospital building. In a small office that smelled like new wool carpeting, a secretary fondled my hundred bucks, last of the Treasure House funds, the very last real money I had, and issued a receipt. "Not refundable," said red printing at its bottom.

"Tape this to your body," she said. "It's the first thing Dr. Carter will need to see in the operating room." I didn't ask about the second thing.

I was to report back at five, a couple hours off, and decided to kill time wandering around the university and the Green. Walking, I tried to make my mind blank as Joy's and just register smells, sights, and sounds. Trees had lost their leaves. Black branches scraggled the air like a photo I once saw of a cleaning lady's nervous system cut from her corpse and spread out like a fan. Noisy college boys, probably clap-soaked like Errol, hustled by me. I sauntered onto the Old Campus, a forest of aged churchlike buildings. Before one stood a life-size bronze statue of Nathan Hale, baby-faced, hands roped behind his back, lips mouthing those sad words that made him famous. Nathan made me remember a display on the Med School's fourth floor in Goldengrove's branch of the State University. As a girl, I wandered up there to gape at bottles of pickled human meat. The tastiest exhibit was John Dillinger's chief henchman, who'd been cooked in the chair, then frozen solid and bandsawed into inch-thick steaks. Some wizard had packed these between slabs of plate glass, to keep them from rotting. You could see every innard, pate to pubic bone.

Wandering through the cool air, I passed a student Secret Society, square windowless stone building like a crypt. Errol insisted members mainly queered each other. God knows what they did, but I didn't care and didn't want to know. Keep wax paper on that dish of rot, and if corpse gas blows it off, well, don't let it happen when I'm nearby holding a match.

Next I knew, I was smack dab in the middle of the state's biggest and oldest cemetery, a gloomy pasture of stiffs whose dust couldn't grow a decent tree, only shriveled, crooked sticks. My reform school had its own little weed-filled graveyard where they dumped girls whose families didn't want the body or have cash to dispose of it. They almost planted Molly Fiddler there. But in spite of the heroic quack who tried to murder her, she survived.

Suddenly it was quarter till five, and I raced back to the hospital to strap on my ticket.

There were four beds in room 358. When I walked in, two of the three teenyboppers I'd talked with were helping each other tie those indecent hospital PJs, way too short and split down the back. It almost broke my heart to see how spindly these children were, scarcely room between their slight, trembling legs for a Kotex. Pulling off my own clothes, stuffing them into an empty locker like in high school, I thought how Dr. Shiflet had crammed soap down Errol's throat, then sliced Errol's neck to let in air.

"I'm like scared," said one child. "Like maybe I'm gonna lie down on a table, you know, and die."

"They don't use knives," I said, shoving my body, bare but for my green ring, into the cold PJs. "Just a sort of Electrolux."

"But they have this needle," said the other child. Both had long straight hair a dead color between blond and brown. Where the hell were their mothers? "I wasn't scared when they took my tonsils out. How come I know I'm gonna die?" Tears trickled down her thin face. "Wish I hadn't of balled Jimmy without no safe."

Afraid myself, I put my arms around her and saw her scrawny neck gray with dirt. "Honey, it's all right."

"I want my mamma," she cried.

"Shurl's mom kicked her out. Shurl's living with me and George."

"How old are you girls?" I asked.

"I'm sixteen," said George's girl. "Shurl's fourteen."

A nurse marched in. Behind her a gangling teen-age attendant wheeled the gurney. "Miss Rogoff?" asked the nurse.

"Me," Shurl sobbed in my arms.

"You don't have to go," I said.

"Like, it's okay." Shurl climbed on the gurney, tugging the rag she wore shut so the lout, all eyeballs, couldn't see her tiny crotch. "Let's, you know, get it over," she told the nurse.

They wheeled her into the hall.

"Does it like breathe any?" asked George's girl.

"What?" I asked.

"Do they have to stick it or something?"

I let myself remember how in reform school, where they locked her away for helping one of her boy friends swipe a car, Molly Fiddler, who was in my barracks, complained one morning that her side hurt. The fatherly quack, highly respected in the Country Club, I'm sure, said it was her appendix and he'd better operate quick. But he waited till Molly's father and the judge who caged her signed a release, though he was in such a rush to cut. Three days later, they carried Molly back into our barracks. Bewilderment cut through her grin of pain.

When the matron left, Molly pulled up her nightie and showed us the plaster on her wound. "Molly," I asked, "how come it's all over?"

"Kid," said a fellow inmate, "they must of took out all your guts."

"Don't know," moaned Molly Fiddler. "They give me a balloon to blow and cut in."

When the bandages came off, it was days before Molly would strip in the light. She lay in bed, covers to her neck, a knotty tightness around her eyes. Then one night she shook me awake in my bunk. Without a word, she lit a match to show what she'd been hiding—on her tiny belly, a cross, each arm a foot long, gouges huge, red, thick-lipped like Jack the Ripper had slashed them with a plow. Molly whimpered, "I don't understand." Who could understand why, with the clank of cutlery, the quack, oozing pus from his beak, had sawed out her ovaries and womb?

When they wheeled Shurl back, smiling through clenched teeth, I had already dressed. I remember an astonished nurse, an elevator's red downlight clanging on. Then I hit the chill evening and scrambled for my car. But only one, black, beat-up, and old, was still parked beneath the smokestacks. Oil stained the pavement like blood where my yellow LTD had stood.

118

CHAPTER *16*

No cop could help me now, no quack or shyster. Had I sheltered myself in the robe of God, he'd have brained me with his crook, grabbed my purse, and raped me. Soon I was stumbling across the Green, feeling that I was heading into time's mirror toward my shack on Pigeon Hill, once again that knocked-up fourteen-year-old buried years deep in my body. A huge, mangy wino shuffled into my path, leering like he knew me well. "Little lady, please." He splayed his giant palm like a platter for my head. "I'm broke!" I yelled, shot around him, and smelled a hot blast from his innards as he shouted filth down on me. I knew something awful, but what?

When I staggered up the porch into my house, Ethel lay on the living-room sofa and scowled at me over mounds of trash. Her look told me that I wouldn't be able to confide in her at all.

"Where's Bess and Jenny?" I panted.

"Never mind," she muttered. "I didn't hear no car pull up. Where's my LTD at?"

"Someone stole it while I was in the hospital. I read in the paper, car thieves are working the place like mad."

"Maybe only towed," Ethel said. "Maybe you done somethin dumb, like park the wrong spot."

"Same thing," I said. "We don't dare ask the cops."

"You always done managed to fuck everthing up," Ethel

growled. Then deep in her guts, an awful whisper, "Filthy little slut."

Her words knocked me square back into the present. "How come you say that, Mamma?"

"Don't play clean an innocent with ol Ethel, whore. You always pretend to know nothin."

"You sick?"

"Fuckin sick. Ever time I see you alive, it makes me toss my cookies. But I'm workin at it."

"At what, Mamma?"

Ethel chuckled, evil and nasty. "Dyin. Dint you know I was gonna die? Won't ever have to see you no more."

"I'm your flesh and blood."

"Ha ha ha."

"If you hate me so much, how come you drove all this way to bring presents?"

"Cause you're so stupid," Ethel snarled, then pressed her belly and groaned.

"Let me run you to the hospital," I said.

"What in?" Ethel moaned. "Wheelbarrow? I'll be okay, you betcha. Ain't finished my work yet." She breathed deeply, took her hands off her belly and slowly sat. "When I get the bellyache, I get like them ads on TV, where this mommy yells at the one she loves most. Then says, Ain't no pissfuck ache gonna make me yell at my loveydovey. An takes them fuckin pills. Yeah. Get your dear ol mom a little white fucker pill, Amelia. Or better, a big, long black fucker, he he. Ain't I my ornery self again?"

"Where are Bess and Jenny?" I asked.

"Bess, she's upstairs takin a leetle nap," Ethel said. "Jenny's out with some man."

"What man?"

Ethel leered. "Ain't gonna spy on my own grandchild."

"She's thirteen," I whispered, feeling my body shake. "Too young for boys."

"Dint look like no boy," Ethel said. "Looked like a full-grown man, big hairy critter cept for his bald head. But you're expert on what's too young. And what ain't."

"Mamma, my God, have you dug *her* up a flying dentist?"

"Wasn't no Piper the two o them took off in."

"That son of a bitch," I sighed, flopping on a musty heap of trash.

"But, sweetie, you sure did a A-One job o gettin even with your dentist, ain't that the truth?"

It was.

That April evening, when I was fourteen and in my fourth month, writhing on our shack's floor among the well-seasoned junk, Ethel had said, "Don't worry, sweetie. I know a doc that jus loves to help young girls." Soon a tall, skinny man, old enough to be my father, walked in, wide-brimmed hat hooding his eyes, thin lips corkscrewed into a scowl, his sliver of mustache like a needle. A black-leather bag dangled from one hand. "Let's get her on the bed," he said. "Don't want her rear to soak up splinters. How many months along?"

"Don't know." Ethel tugged my ankles, the flying dentist manhandled my armpits. "I wasn't in the back seat when she caught this foul ball."

"Where's her daddy?"

"When he took off, it wasn't no forwarding address he left behind."

The flying dentist pulled off my clothes. "Mighty well developed for her age," he said.

"Oh, mighty well," Ethel agreed.

"Easy there, dear," the flying dentist said, wine thick on his breath. "This infant's gonna deliver. Yeah. There she blows. Gimme a towel. Don't want this little wound bleeding too much. Maybe— No. It's dead. Hand over some news-papers. String."

"Looks like a goddamn war," Ethel said. "All that crud."

"She'll pull through," the flying dentist said.

"Bet you'd like that, Doc. Easy there, sweetie. Your sins ain't all caught up with you yet. Give em time. Doc, better take the married man's stitch. Make 'er snug and tight."

I had a man four weeks later, when I was almost too sore yet to walk, a National Guard sergeant on bivouac near Goldengrove, who gave me a deuce, then put his platoon onto me. I was keeping the wound open, or trying to heal it the only way I knew. Then the flying dentist, whose son was in high school with me, got around to gouging his fee.

He parked his airplane in a hangar at Kister's Field. I'd strap myself in. Before takeoff he'd spoon liquid into my mouth, syrupy and cherry-flavored, so I wouldn't care which cavity he was filling.

The flying dentist had a wife, naturally. A respected pillar of society, he was serving his third term as president of the Goldengrove Country Club. While he was about his clumsy business in that tight cockpit, he kept slobbering, "Oh, I love you, little girl." I thought one way I might heal myself was scissor my legs in midflight. Then his foul blood would scab the tenderness inside me, help form a tough hide like my outer body, leave me whole.

This carried on through much of my sophomore year, when I began dating the flying dentist's son. This was the year of my popularity, straight A's, student council and the like. And he was a senior, football quarterback, basketball center, president of his class. One of those big deals in high school who later flunked college and never amounted to cat litter. At last his old man set him up in a Shell station, catercorner from Goldengrove High, the year some arsonist sent it up in flames. They never caught the person who set that fire.

His old man cracked with jealousy when he found his son and I were going out. He hollered, threatened. But I said, "Sure. Try and do anything, then see what happens."

I relished the evening when the kid drove me home in his daddy's Buick Eight to meet his parents. He and I, his mom and the flying dentist sat around the living room making polite talk, and I showed my calves and knees, and stuck my bubs hard against my sweater. The whole time, the flying dentist ground his molars, hands clamped like plumber's friends over his filthy crotch. Leaving, I ignored the paw he stuck out for me to shake.

He stopped threatening, because it didn't work, and started paying me. He'd beaten the tax people raw, he boasted. When clients paid cash, he gouged only half his fee, and had taken to burying his hoard all over the back lawn, in

Mason jars, which he sealed full of greenbacks the way you seal peaches. "Squeeze him till he shits green," Ethel said. So I inflated the value of poontang to a sealed quart jar, payable before takeoff. I'd refuse the next date with his son, I said, if the flying dentist dredged up a second quart. Finally I said plain out it would cost one Mason jar per week, without nookey, to keep me from ratting to his wife. "Blackmail!" he cried.

"You blackhearted bastard," I said. "Get out your shovel and dig."

Finally I came clean to the son. Parked with him in the flying dentist's Buick Eight on a back road which led to the quarry, I confessed a whole packet of sins, though I left his daddy out. "Liar!" the boy shouted. "Whore!" Suddenly, a wildcat was clawing into my pants. I scratched and kicked till he whimpered bleeding behind the big wheel. "Drive me home, Jasper," I said.

Next day, I called IRS. If they wanted to hook a shark, I said without giving my name, take shovels two miles past the Country Club on State Road 6 and dig for worms. The flying dentist pled guilty, there was no way out. They gave him a year and a day, with a week off to clear up his affairs. Jesus, it was good to get him!

Then suddenly Ethel disappeared, no word, no note. That midnight, the sheriff and a half dozen deputies busted down my door. Like a mole, the sheriff burrowed into Ethel's trashpile. "Here it is, real stuff, goddamn it!" He waved a thick green pad, then stuffed it into his pocket. They hauled me to jail. Next day, the sheriff trotted me before a judge and charged me with theft, vagrancy, being suspicious, living alone in a condemned dwelling. From the baseboard like big cockroaches came a dozen high school boys, pimply and greasy. They oozed onto the stand squeaking they "had relations" with me single and as a group. I was charged with being promiscuous and indecent. The judge, another pillar of society, who specialized in ax and block, sent me packing to reform school for "an indefinite period," to heal the deep wounds in my soul.

I decided on the spot that society could screw itself, that

I would lie and steal, and worse, do anything to keep from holding a "respectable job." In however large or small a way, I'd avenge myself against judges and sheriffs and flying dentists, pillars of society who built my cage.

Now someone pounded my door. In walked Jenny, slender and smiling, followed by a very clean old man, pole-thin, in a blue suit, arms like tubes, pants like swords. Well, if anybody ever felt vornated!

And though I should have been relieved, I wasn't at all.

"If it isn't Dr. Shiflet," I said.

Then I lit into Ethel. "Did you know Jenny was out with her own grandpa?"

"Ohhh, my guts," Ethel groaned.

"You old crook. As if I haven't suffered enough."

"What on earth is the trouble here?" Dr. Shiflet's bedside voice, low and sugary, sounded like a fat fee already heated his butt. "Why should such a lovely woman sound so upset?"

"Which lovely woman you talking bout, sweetie?" Ethel's red pig eyes fired Dr. Shiflet a coy squint.

"Why, I see three lovely ladies in this room."

"Grandfather and I had a conversation," Jenny said.

My juices cooled. "What about?"

"Daddy," Jenny said. "Daddy's fish. Grandmother Shiflet, who stayed in Columbus. And Grandfather's snakes."

"She's maturing into an intelligent as well as a very slender young woman," Dr. Shiflet said, sucking in all the living room's trash with his cold blue peepers. "I'm sure Jenny remembers the thrust of our conversation."

"Grandfather wants me to come live in Columbus," Jenny said.

"Upper Arlington," Dr. Shiflet added, "where the best people are. Because I've just retired from practice, I'll have time to oversee the upbringing of this young lady. She needs a man's firm hand, and that son of mine clearly can't provide it."

"Who's bringing up your snakes while you're here?" I asked.

"Wife." Dr. Shiflet licked his thin lips.

"Jenny, what's your opinion of vipers for brothers and sisters?"

"Now now," Dr. Shiflet said. "I'm not trying to thrust myself on anyone. I am a bit thirsty, though."

And suddenly, like through a telescopic sight, I saw the bull's eye in his self-control, and in his billfold.

"You done a fine job raisin that there Errol," Ethel butted in. "He's so big an strong. My daughter sure fucked up lettin that'un slip."

"Errol," said Dr. Shiflet, "is an enormous disappointment."

"Ain't he a doctor, too?" Ethel asked.

"With a great deal of concentrated effort," said Dr. Shiflet, "Errol managed to geld his career. Now the main thrust of his life is debauchery."

"Rest yer sawbones, Doctor." Ethel waved toward a stack of well-seasoned newspapers. "Tell us bout the thrust of more things."

"What thrust?" asked Dr. Shiflet, truly bewildered.

I saw my opening and said, "I'll hustle some wine. So the doctor'll know this is a friendly camp."

My dirt-floored basement stank so, a whole zoo could be using it for a privy. In a cool corner lay the last three bottles of stolen wine, which Billy Graham said tasted like nectar. I wanted to break Dr. Shiflet's old bald head like an eggshell. Lord knows he wasn't worth his weight in dead cats, but what had he done to make me so murderous?

Upstairs, Dr. Shiflet and Ethel had already grown chummy. ". . . gonna be mighty disappointed," Ethel was saying, punch line of some joke. Dr. Shiflet hollered, "Haw haw!" Looking blank, Jenny leaned against the mantel like a sponge in chilly water, soaking it all in.

"That'un always was old Casey's favorite," Ethel snorted.

Ethel's mood had swung completely from sour to sweet, a trapeze act she had been performing often of late. Sometimes she'd sit still whole hours at a time, and a mellow smile would stretch her little mouth. When I asked what she was thinking, she'd respond oddly. "The end's gonna burn my whole life clean." Or, "It's wonderful how nothin matters a-tall." She was like a story I read in the paper about a skydiver whose chute didn't open, but who somehow survived. When he knew he was about to get splattered, all at once every happy moment of his life poured through his mind, and when he hit the ground his mood was so sweet and golden, it was a terrible disappointment waking in that hospital bed still alive.

Now I handed the bottle to Dr. Shiflet.

Freezing the label with his cold eyes, he asked, "How the devil did you come by this?"

"Why, I made it myself, Doctor," I said.

"Château" something-or-other "1937," he read aloud, like the world's greatest poem. "Never thought I'd live to see it. Have you"—he could hardly bring it out—"a corkscrew?"

"Jam in the cork with a knife handle," I said.

He winced, like the cork was to be jammed down his throat, but said, "Get the knife. Quick. And a very clean wineglass."

"How about a jellyglass?" I asked.

"The fountainhead of wines," he murmured, shaking his head slowly, "flowing in this dung..eap. Let's free this luscious creature from her past."

"Save your poor sore mom the trouble, Jenny," I said. She left for the kitchen. Dr. Shiflet carefully peeled away the coat of lead. Mold crusted the cork. "Ah!" he sighed. "Sad we can't savor this cork. It'll stay there till the glass breaks."

If he was so concerned, why not hop over to any supermarket and pick up a thirty-five-cent corkscrew? But the good doctor lusted too hotly. Jenny returned with a butter knife and a glass. Gingerly Dr. Shiflet thrust the cork down into the bottle's throat. A rich fruity scent cut the stink of trash.

"Wow!" I cried out. "Thought it might be rotten."

"All that ambrosial past!" he sighed.

"Hoo boy." Ethel looked sad. "Some fungus must of crawled in my old wine bottle way back."

French wine ticky-tocked. When the cork floated free behind the bottle's shoulders, purple bled into the tumbler. "Should air it two hours." Plainly he didn't intend on airing it a half minute. He sniffed, eyeballs rolling like death, then he swooshed some in his cheeks like mouthwash. With a piggy grunt, he swallowed. "Aagh!" he gasped, like he'd come in his pants.

"How does that stack up," I asked, "with Ivory soap?"

Dr. Shiflet swooned with delight. "I can't believe that it's really what the label says. But it is."

I said, "When you're raising Jenny with that man's firm hand, what razor blades will you use? They've got these platinum jobbies that cut sharper than steel."

"Have a little decency, will you?" Dr. Shiflet muttered, sipping.

Some people never learn a damn thing from their past. "Give me that bottle!" I grabbed it from his old paws and drank. Tart, with the tang of baby's spit, cool and alive, it blanketed my tongue. Right off, I felt its soft kick in my brain.

"Not from the bottle!" yelled Dr. Shiflet.

"It's *my* bottle!"

"Amelia," Ethel said. "Doctor, out in that kitchen a sec. Take Jenny. Me an my girl need to chat."

"God, wine!" But he rose, having no choice, took Jenny's hand, and slithered out.

"Honey," Ethel whispered, "this is your big chance. Don't blow it."

"What is?" I swilled the dark cream.

"This fucker's rich. Play him right, milk him dry."

Giving her a huge wink, I called, "Dr. Shiflet, scoot back, now." The old gristle-chunk could have set a record on the salt flats.

I swung the half-empty bottle like a pendulum before his hungry eyes. "Oh!" he said. "No!"

"The sands are running out." I gurgled more wine.

"Gaagh!" He strained like a dog with a peach pit locked in its butt.

"Lose control of yourself," I told him quietly. "Blow

127

apart, Doctor, show me what you really are. Then maybe I'll feed you a few last drops of blood."

"Goddamn!" he shouted. "Shit! Who the fuck—*bitches!*" He reared on his hind legs, turned purple, clenched his hairy fists till fingernails cut his palms. *"Fucking shit!"*

Jenny lounged in the doorway and placidly watched. "What on earth is wrong with Grandfather?"

"Nothing," I said. "Grandpa just dropped his mask."

"It's for sure," said Ethel mournfully, "that now he ain't gonna drop nothin o value."

"Men," Jenny said. "They're all alike."

"I haven't had much luck with them," I agreed.

"Shit!" yelled Dr. Shiflet.

"Pore man's got apoplexy," Ethel said.

"Yes. Settle down, Dr. Shiflet," I murmured into his raging storm. "Here." I poured into his tumbler the last wine, and held it before his purple face.

Finally he brought it into focus, stopped yelling, and sobbed like a baby. "I'm such a fool." His skinny shoulders shook. Like a buzzard, he settled back on Ethel's trash.

I handed him the glass. "Drink. Take your time." As the glass trembled to his lips, I patted the bony skeleton of his back.

"Hope you ladies can forgive me," he sobbed.

I went into the kitchen. When I came back, I dangled the last two bottles before his guilty eyes.

"Will you take a check?" he asked, pawing like a spastic for the inside of his coat.

"It's all right," I said, limp and golden inside, strange from the grape. "Take your time. Everything's going to be just fine."

CHAPTER *17*

"Fine" was a check for $400, an Rx Dr. Shiflet simply scratched down without haggling or even being asked. Guilt money, I suppose, a medicine that should have kept us well for a reasonable time, if it hadn't been for having to pay the undertaker.

In December the weather got sick. One day it was summer, near eighty. Chickadees and grackles, sparrows and starlings, poor dears, thought it really was mating season and went wild on those barren boughs, squawking with horniness, while sap flooded up the tree trunks. That night the half moon shivered crisp and still, a dry-ice scrap steaming with frosty mist. Before the cold sun rose, the temperature dropped to zero. By noon a blizzard hit, a low hissing. Birds died. Huge trees, completely faked out, blew open like plugged pressure cookers. And my body, which is usually smarter than my mind, started acting like a fool. I squirmed around the whole icy day feeling so sex-crazed I could die.

Toward supper, I shot a letter to Lonzo, my only one since he wrote in September. "Dear Funlover, Merry Christmas! Hope you are having a wonderful time all cooped up in a little cell, as I am free as a bird in the outside world. I also hope that those black boys have not yet robbed you of your sterling virtue, though it seems to me that is your only chance for action. Maybe you should not let it slip through your fingers. Next time in the shower, remember that TV ad which says you only pass this way once, so grab all the gusto you can, ha ha.

"Seriously, Lonzo, there were some pretty hairy moments when I found out the alimony, which was sorely needed, would not come in. And now Santa may show up with only a switch and a lump of coal for the girls. As for the cause of your trouble, I felt a mite angry, though of course all is forgiven now. When are you going to learn that it is *impossible* for an eight-year-old girl to be anybody's grandma? Maybe you had better see an eye doctor for Buford, the one-eyed worm, whose size you take such great pride in, and improve its aim.

"You will be happy to hear that I am having a ball. Mamma Ethel has come to visit. As you know she has always had a steadying influence on my life. And though she is peaked and not up to her full orneryness, I am in great shape and can do enough for two. Just recently she's taken to sitting around in a trance. When she finally snaps out, she tells me how golden and peaceful she feels inside. Don't know what's wrong with old Ethel. Maybe she needs another operation on her belly. She always has needed a doctor to cut the mud vein out of her mind. I've got a big problem with my own body, which you seem to like a lot now that you are locked up and pickings are slim. But I won't name it here, because you would get jealous. To keep you from worry, I'll save it as a present for when next we meet, however many years off. Why we keep repeating the same dumb actions beats me completely.

"Bess grows more wild every day. Marlene has run off with a boy who reminds me of you, he's such a hick. So far as I know she is living in his apartment. Marlene has offered to help me get back on the tracks. But it seems bassackward for a child to mother her own parent, as Ethel always used to burden me with her men and diseases.

"I sure hope it's given you a lift to hear from the outside world. Though I suppose you get love letters from your harem, not to mention small children, pining away till you walk through those prison gates, the same old Lonzo. You ask about help I might be able to give toward saving you. Maybe

130

if I get my own house in order, you will indeed see my smiling face in Christmas ribbons reaching down to haul you out of your sinkhole, by my teeth, I suppose, like a circus freak. Then we can work a sideshow.

Your ex-wife,
Amelia Biggs

P.S. Got laid yet by the warden's 'hot wife,' as you put it, who sneaked out your last letter to me?"

No sooner had I stomped back inside the house after trudging through four-foot snowdrifts to post my letter, than the phone rang. A sad, small voice said, "Amelia? Errol."

"What's up?"

"Oh, Lord, if I've ever needed help in my miserable life, I need it now. Goddamn those psychopaths and their callow lack of compassion! By God"—the old fury seeped into his voice—"kids don't know how suffering feels. That's why they're the most idiotic drivers in the world! Because they've never felt a goddamn thing!"

"What happened, Errol? Somebody bash in your fender?"

"They threw me out!" Errol howled. "They pitched my Red Devil into a snowbank!"

"Where you calling from?"

"I managed to drive four miles. But the goddamn Highway Department hasn't plowed the back roads. My Morris skidded into a drift. Walked to this phone booth on the Post Road. It's the only shelter I have."

"Can't your old man help?"

"That pustule already popped back to Columbus."

"Errol, I hope you don't expect to stay with me. Why don't you call Joy?"

Wind at his end of the line whooped. "Did already," he finally said. "Michael's still at the library with their car. Look, when they find my body after the spring thaw, don't blame yourself."

"Have they plowed Post Road?" I asked.

"Yes. I'm at Cranmont. Southeast corner. But don't bother."

Ethel called from the head of the stairs, "Where you off

to this time?" Since getting a mysterious phone call the night before, she'd been complaining that she felt like death. But she wouldn't tell me who had called, or what her problem was.

"Errol's freezing to death," I said.

"That ol fishfuck. How come he dint call Joy? Should o seen them two dryhumpin on Jenny's birthday."

"Ridiculous," I said. "Errol has clap."

"When a gal feels like doin the tango," Ethel said, "she don't ask the bandleader if his baton's been in the washer. If you can spare a minute from rescuin Errol, look in on ol Ethel. Her worthless life might need savin, too."

"Drink some Pepto-Bismol," I said, and slammed out.

Lonzo's '57 Chevy was a curbside igloo. When I batted it with my gloved hands, freezing powder whooshed into my face, puffed up my coat sleeves. Hot needles of ice pricked my wrists. Finally I cleared the windows and climbed in, only to find that a fine talcum had sifted everywhere. Dusting a clear spot for my bottom, I stuck in my key, and the old engine turned over, pow. I wondered how the bastard that stole the LTD was getting along in this cold, but figured he was probably part of some Mafia ring, which pulled it to pieces and shipped them to Miami, where Florida crooks stuck together hunks of a hundred different cars. I imagined that the LTD had multiplied into a whole guilty fleet, chauffeured for rich honchos near scalding, sandy beaches.

I didn't have snow tires, just the baldies on there when Lonzo gave me the car. When I shifted to drive, the hulk shivered in place, back wheels whirling, then slowly took off, a seaworthy tub on snow other cars had packed down during the day. If the antifreeze, which, like the tires, had been around since year 1, still held out, I could siphon some off for Errol, like the booze St. Bernards carry in the Alps. The heater fan rattled, then wound to a steady whir, and the car warmed fast as I drove over ice and snow to save Errol.

I'd been coming this way often to steal from the rich and give to ailing Ethel, who always asked, where did I filch this thing? what houses, what address did this one come from? as if she wanted to dream her old sick self into those fine houses with me, before turning the loot over to Billy Graham. "Lord knows what Ethel's got, maybe the disease that killed all them ellums," I heard Billy grumbling once, thinking of the huge Dutch elms that once shaded Elm City. When Errol, little Marlene, and I first moved here, a few still stood, thick-bolled and golden in autumn. But the very next spring, when oaks and maples were squeezing out their delicate floss, most elms already clawed the bright-blue sky in death. No poison could save them.

Spelunking those empty summer hulks near Errol's commune, I found that even the rich are packrats. One whole huge dirt-floored basement was crammed to the ceiling with a paradise of old newspapers, a maze with corridors spidering out from the cold furnace, as if Ethel had once lived there. Maybe by storing up all life's newspapers, the person thought he or she was keeping every day alive in the bank. The worst place I broke into broke every possible fire code. This house was crammed with empty paint cans, mildewed garbage, balled Christmas paper, withered fruit rinds, empty bottles. You could hear the roaches mate. What possessed people? Loneliness? Fear of emptiness—if only they filled it, they could burrow like a mole and be safe? Maybe self-love rubbed off even on their watermelon rinds and crap, and gave it value, the way gold rubs off on greenbacks. Or like keepsakes, the corncob a man loves because he's smoked it filthy for forty years, Cracker Jack prizes, bubblegum cards, all blown out to fill the universe. And you squat at the center, rat eyes bugging, whiskers twitching, Lord of Creation.

In every house, I left a poem signed "Cat Burglar."

Driving to save Errol from frostbite got me remembering when, newlyweds, we moved to Elm City and Errol started teaching at the university. His chairman, Charles, invited the new young faculty to his mansion, for dinner with Deedee, his wife, Elm City's true queen of cultcha. They owned a feebleminded Great Dane. Every few minutes Deedee crowed, "Chahls! Take Misty out! She must make a poo!" Misty dropped a ton of poo for us, white-haired, dimpled old Chahls holding her vast paw each time. In the middle of dinner, I saw Deedee's long coral claw pick her nose, and I wondered if she could possibly be anybody's mother.

Deedee packratted brand-name paintings. Her walls had room for only a fraction of what she owned, so stacked canvases filled half their basement. With her yellow teeth, she owned half of Southern New England Bell. Chahls himself came into the marriage with a fat wad, buying a lifetime of grade A misery, because, raunchy as low-class Ethel, Deedee also packratted colleagues of Chahls's, so he'd feel at home in the Faculty Club, smelling dried Deedee over the soup and nuts. I'm ashamed to say, I wanted to give Misty rabies, then watch googoo-eyed while she snapped her mistress into stringy hunks.

That night, Chahls got pie-eyed and told his starving peons, "For the privilege of teaching at Elm City University, you should be glad to live on the Green in a puptent." Barreling home, Errol choked on bile. "Yaaaah! Chahls teethed on a rubber dildo! He's worse than my old man. He jacks off daydreaming of cockroaches and spiders! A ten-pound blind albino iguana lives in his colon!"

Now my headlights smeared yellow on Errol, homeless and puptentless, shivering behind the phone booth's frosty panes. Thinking of those spy movies, where some desperate spy, phoning for help, fields a pound of lead through the glass, I didn't brake in time. The baldies wouldn't grab ice, I slid toward the booth, and seeing me bear down Errol froze with fear and only luck blocked me six inches from creaming him.

"Jesus H. Christ!" He flung open my door. "I asked you to save me, goddamn it, not plow me under ten kilograms of broken glass!"

"Will you please climb in?" I asked him calmly.

It was snowing again, so hard my headlights looked like they were shining into a mirror. "The cruelty of children," Errol said. "Even you wouldn't have thrown out an innocent fish."

"Don't goad me when I'm doing you a favor."

"Only to buy off your guilt," Errol said. "You're why they threw me out. Ah well," he sighed. "That Red Devil chewed

134

a hunk out of Bill's hand before he could throw her loose. Must have been stoned to the gills, reaching into the tank. Blood in the water, blood all over the snow. But I couldn't find her. Still, those fuckers have nine lives. Maybe I can dig her out before the thaw."

"You're plain crazy," I said, then had a sudden thought. "Errol, are you the Cat Burglar?"

"Lord help me! I'm no more the Cat Burglar," Errol said, "than you are."

Which only kept me wondering.

While I worked the plutocratic booneys, the Cat Burglar busied himself at the center of Elm City, where work was risky and pickings were slim. With every break-in, he became more reckless, striking a small pizza parlor on the lit-up Green, smoking through a pack of fags in its weenie john, fixing a large garbage pie with anchovies, and eating a precise quarter of it, plastering a poem to the plate-glass door, and sauntering out with $2.56 in loose change. My unworldly young instructor called it "art for art's sake," then harangued us about how all great artists are criminals. But now the Cat Burglar was having trouble with publication because the poems had grown so filthy, a strong reason I suspected Errol. For a while, the paper would leave the filth to the reader's imagination:

> I'm wishing that I had the luck
> To steal a flying wild ——!
> But —— it all, I've had a fit:
> My pocket's only filled with ——!

Some evil-minded readers who thought they knew the missing words raised such a stink that the paper stopped printing anything of his. The editor was even inspired to write the Cat Burglar an open letter wishing "you would find more useful channels through which to pour your hitherto tragically perverted talents," and suggesting, "You might make an honest fortune writing your adventures into a best seller."

Soon after, he did pour his perverted talent into another

channel—Western Union—phoning a telegram from a burglary straight to the police, and charging it to the victim's number.

The Cat Burglar was so much on my mind I'd dreamed about him. The thing emerged small and black from Liggett's and crossed Church Street to the Green, furious and jerky like the rabid dog I saw my daddy kill with one blast of his twelve-gauge Savage. No cars, no breeze rustled the midnight trees whose roots tangled with human bones. The Cat Burglar trembled with epilepsy, huge black tail shaking like a tree limb in a storm. Its mouth foamed, its elbows flapped throwing shadows like wings all across the Green. Slowly it rose above Elm City, sucking blind clouds of dust off the street. Up it flew over the businesses, the university, the three churches, over the whole town asleep like death. Like that night on the beach after I robbed my Treasure House, I felt this dream touched against something real.

At my curb, I eased the Chevy to rest behind another car.

"Michael must've come back," Errol said. "Isn't that Joy's Cougar?"

"How come they're here?"

"Probably because Joy knew I was calling you for help."

"Do you think I give a damn what filth goes on between you two? Go scat!"

Errol stumbled into a growing blizzard. I let him walk ahead. Damned if I wanted to touch his trail of live clap before it froze.

Stomping inside and slapping the snow off me, I saw a prayer meeting around the couch. Errol and Joy Silverspring looked on silently. Michael and Billy Graham knelt. On the first stair step sat little Bess and beside her, Jenny held baby Axel, all three still as ice cakes.

"Looks like family night at the Salvation Army," I said.

"It's old Ethel," said Billy Graham. "She ain't too dern good."

"Aw." A little squeak from Ethel. "Jus spoon in 'leven peter, I'll come round."

"Two Peter," Michael said.

136

"Feel peaceful," Ethel squeaked. "Ain't worried bout a thing."

"What were you and Errol doing together?" Joy Silverspring snapped at me.

"Joy," I said, "you're the only woman I know able to clap with both hands tied."

"Sounds o strife," Ethel whispered. "Don't hardly hold a grudge no more. Like I done forgot the past."

"Joy can't remember hers either," I said. "She was so wildly happy."

"O Lethe!" Errol said.

Ethel whispered, "All you stop fightin."

"I don't understand what Amelia meant by clapping." Joy looked dead into Errol's eyes and hugged herself tight. "What low humor lies behind it?"

"I'll tell you," Errol muttered sheepishly. "Later."

"Mamma, didn't you take that Pepto-Bismol?" I asked.

"The whole bah-ul ain't gonna help Ethel," said Billy Graham.

"Honeypie," Ethel sighed, "I'm a goner."

"Slow down a minute," I said. "You're leaving me behind."

"My grandmother," said Jenny from the stairs, "is very ill."

"Good God, don't wake Axel," Joy snapped.

"I'm at peace," Ethel sighed. "For the first time in my whole dang life. Ain't that a down-an-out scream?"

"Hold my Good Book." Michael flopped it into her face.

"Michael, you sick prick," Joy muttered.

"Use the dang thing for wiping ass," Ethel said. "If there's any fuckhead God, he's gonna drop me to hell no matter what, an I don't care, I feel so dang fine right now."

"I felt that hopped up once," Billy Graham said, "in a Hong Kong opium den."

"Wait'll ya die," Ethel told him. "Ya got a real treat comin."

"Mamma, you're not going to die," I said. "What'll I do?"

"Put me in pine," said Ethel, "an pay the unnertaker cold cash. Shit, honey, I ain't even got roun yet to finishin up the errand I come on. Always was halfhearted bout it, though. And it don't matter now."

"Cheapest funeral costs more'n a hunnerd smackeroos." Billy shook his cruddy old head. "Course, that ain't nothing to what the bah-ul of nitrogen's gonna cost when I kick off. Whew! Better get to work quick and get the dough together before I die."

"Mamma." I felt a great fear rising. I didn't want to ask, but I felt safer with people around. "What errand did you come on?"

"I was wondering the very same thing," Jenny said, cradling the child.

"For God's sake! Axel!" Joy hissed.

"Don't you know?" Ethel asked. "Don't you even remember? Well, no matter. It come from evil in the heart, an I don't feel nothin like that no more a-tall. Just gimme smiles o love an forgiving."

I was close enough to hear Joy whisper in Errol's ear, "If you fucked her, so help me God I don't care what I do tonight! It'll be all over the front page of tomorrow's paper!"

Like a cherry bomb blew off in his didie, Axel roared, "Yaaaaaagh!"

"Oh, Jesus," Joy said.

"That Axel." Michael shook his head wearily.

Where the blue robe covered Ethel's lap, I saw a stain widening like the projectionist had hit the wrong button, speeding the film till it melted from whizzing. "Mamma, you're wetting yourself."

"Ain't," Ethel said.

"Ghaaaaaargh!" Axel roared.

The stain looked red as a dead leaf. It soaked the couch.

"Take me somewheres quiet," Ethel whispered.

"University Hospital." I grabbed her under the arms. "Michael? Billy? Help me get her to the car, she's gushing blood!"

138

"Don't nobody touch me but Amelia," Ethel said. "Nobody!"

I tugged Ethel to her feet. "Wrap that coat round her shoulders! Errol, goddamn it, get the car open, scoot!"

"Bossy!" Joy said.

Axel's giant horn vibrated.

Mamma and I stumbled into the hissing blizzard, plunged knee-deep through the snow to the car. Not till we both got in did I see that her feet were bare. A thick, black trail like a mud vein had followed us.

"Ain't gonna save my life," Ethel whispered. "Don't even try. My peach Buster got ahold of me by phone last night. Judas has done sold out to the pigs. Jig's up."

My bald rear tires whined and smoked as we sailed onto the white street.

I tore through stop signs, homing in my mind on the huge twin smokestacks. At the Green's north edge, I plowed through my first red light.

"No use riskin yer own life to try an save mine," Ethel said. "Never did come here on no errand o mercy."

The rotten windshield wipers barely whooshed aside tons of violent snow. Christmas lights were winking and blinking all over the Green.

"Why'd you come?" I felt the fear. A stop light up ahead marked the Green's south edge.

"I forgive you," sighed Ethel. "Don't matter a-tall no more. But you don't even remember? Really?"

Headlights knifed toward the intersection.

"Revenge," Ethel whispered. "For what you an Casey—"

Before the emerald stoplight, a car's brights blazed in front of me. Swerving to miss them, I slammed a light pole. Only the steering wheel kept me from flying through the windshield. Snow poured through a hole in the glass onto the empty seat beside me.

I staggered out my door. The car that caused the accident hadn't stopped. Not even its tire tracks marked the snowy road, only mine, leading to the stainless steel post. Antifreeze dribbled from the crumpled Chevy. Torn chin to crotch, Ethel lay spreadeagled barefoot on her back under the green light in an intersection white with virgin snow. I ran, knelt, grabbed her body in my arms. Her mouth had shrunk to a babe's. Somewhere in midair the teeth had fallen out. I looked into her red, happy eyes. While hot blood melted the snow and made a frozen puddle there, we waited for the cops to come along.

CHAPTER *18*

I still cradled Ethel when at last the buttons cruised in, red light whirling. Then came a car, with a newspaper photographer, who flashed bulb after bulb into my face, as if he'd happened on a juicy war atrocity here in the middle of downtown Elm City. By the time three ambulances from three competing undertakers whooshed up at once, she'd gone cold in my arms. The drivers launched into a battle about whose the prize was. While two shoved each other, the third snuck over to me and got down to business. Stretcher boys loomed above me like snowmen. I stood, dripping blood, and watched them cart Ethel off.

Then the fuzz arrested me.

"That was my own mamma," I sobbed.

"All the more reason to drive carefully, lady." The cop, a tall, skinny smiler, was taking me to the emergency room.

"She was gushing blood," I said. "I was rushing her to the hospital."

"Didn't make it, did you," said the cop.

"Car almost rammed me head on. I had to swerve."

"Lady, that street's one-way," the cop said. "No car tracks but yours."

"Snow must've—"

"Snow didn't cover *your* tracks, lady," the cop said.

Cops crammed the E.R.'s waiting room and hall, shepherding citizens in pain, gore painting them like black tallow. I wondered if there'd been a battle someplace. But where blood was the contest, I took blue ribbon. One huge buck, gift-wrapped in a turban of bloody gauze, looked down my front and said, "Whew! Honey, you be the biggest mess I ever saw!"

My button sat me beside three pretty black teen-agers, sobbing like their hearts were split. The cop with them wore a shit-eating grin, so the one with me asked, "Jones, wha-chew got?"

"Man give all three a ride," Jones said, "parks in the boondocks, draws a gun—"

"Hey?"

"When he's done, he shoots water on their heads and gives his blessing."

"That prick," my cop said. "The one pretending to be a priest?"

"His M.O.," Jones agreed. "Lucky as hell we haven't nailed him yet. Crazy bastard's gone hog-wild."

"Because them Catholics don't let their preachers get hitched."

You boobs wouldn't consider it such a joke if he took a crack at your wives, I thought.

"What happened," my cop went on, "all the fathers met in secret and picked one to do it by proxy for everybody. Enormous job."

"Oh, enormous," Jones agreed.

A young resident, who thought I was bleeding to death, took me at once. But when I lay naked on the table, he poked around and said, "You're fine. Whose blood is this?"

"Mamma's. She died in a wreck."

He felt my pooching tummy. "How far along?"

"Four months. She's almost big enough to kick."

"Better keep you for observation. You might lose him."

"I've been eyeballed enough for one lifetime," I said. "Besides, the fuzz wants to arrest me."

"Lie here." The resident marched out. "Did you know this woman is pregnant?" I heard him shout. "Be reason-

142

able!" He came back after a while. "Those cops give me a pain in the stethoscope. I'll write down the name and phone of a lawyer, buddy of mine. Say Rope recommended him. Rope's my nickname. He graduated first in his class last year from Elm City Law School. Editor of the *Journal*. Woman in your condition shouldn't be hassled."

Scrawled on a prescription form, the name was William Robert Ball, Jr. There were two phone numbers.

My clothes, plus coat, were gummed with Ethel's blood, so the hospital gave me a blue, starchy orderly's dress and a blanket to throw over my shoulders. Heater blowing, the cop drove around the Green to the ancient red-brick police station, beside the post office, and helped me into the dingiest cavern I'd entered since reform school, yellow walls, yellow light bulbs hanging by long, frayed cords. The air was stifling damp, as if a whole squadron of fuzz had pissed on white-hot radiators. After sitting me by one of fifty desks and filling out a form, the cop told me my rights.

A thick, strong-looking man in a shiny blue suit wandered over. "Mrs. Biggs, I'm Sergeant Wilson," he said. "Like to ask some questions, if you don't mind." Sitting on the desk's edge, he hulked above me. A huge weapon bulged under his armpit.

"My own mamma just died in my arms while I was rushing to save her life," I said. "And I might lose my baby."

"She's pregnant?" he asked my cop. I noticed that the first joint of Wilson's ring finger was missing.

"Have you ever had a child?" I asked.

"Grown daughter," he muttered. "So you're pregnant?"

"That's what the doctor said," the cop told him.

"I have a lawyer," I said. "William Robert Ball, Jr."

"Bobby Ball is one gung-ho soldier," my lanky cop chuckled.

"Toy soldier." Wilson grinned, showing a gap between his front teeth. "Mrs. Biggs, what was your mother's last name? We've ordered an autopsy on her, by the way."

"Dollarhide. Quit acting like I'm some murderess."

"Dollarhide." Wilson looked at the splintery floor, pleasant face seamed and fatherly. "No chance she remarried recently?"

"Dollarhide," I repeated.

"Ah, how long had she been visiting you?" He acted like he already knew something tasty, but was keeping mum.

"Years."

"I see." Sergeant Wilson's bright-brown eyes were butting smack dab against mine. "All right, Mrs. Biggs. You've had a rough night. Shall we call your husband to pick you up?"

"I'm a divorced woman."

"Then I'll drive you home myself."

"Rather my neighbors didn't see me in a cop car," I sniffed.

"Mine's unmarked." He clumped out of the yellow room a moment, then strode back, big grizzly throwing on a trenchcoat lined with sheep, Stetson screwed like a helmet to his skull. "Let's brave the cold, little lady," he said. "By the way, the name's Bill."

Wind howled across the Green as Sergeant Wilson knocked snow off a bunged-up Ford. No doubt he was a poor workingman, doing an honest job while blowing out a few brains along the way. And suddenly the miserable storm blew a thought into my head. "Hey, Bill! Mamma's teeth fell out in that wreck. We got to find them."

"Gonna have a pretty rough old time." We creaked onto Church Street and headed around the Green's south side. "We'll have to plot her trajectory from the pole. Loved your mother?"

"She was my only mamma."

"And what about your father?"

I felt an ice block round my heart, and below that a bonfire that had no business burning. "Oh, dead!" I cried out. "Dead for years and years!"

The Chevy had been towed. One sign of the deathly accident remained: in the steel pole where no snow stuck, a bright dent.

144

In the blizzard, I tugged the blanket tight round me while we rummaged and kicked through the drifts. What was I really looking for, I wondered, since Ethel was far happier with her choppers out? Because of my crazy state, I suddenly felt that the plastic fangs might fly out of the snow and chomp me like bulldog jaws. I recalled those nightmare comic books, "Crypt of Horror" and "Vault of Terror," where the dead come back, bones poking through skin, to get revenge. And I hoped some truck had rumbled over Ethel's teeth, smashing them. A toothless Ethel terrified me less than an Ethel with fangs in place. My daddy told me he once saw someone spear a moray eel. But when the man tugged it off his barbs, the monster snapped away his hand. Only Casey Dollarhide's superquick reflexes saved the stranger's life, though it cost Casey two more fingers. "Bill Wilson!" I shouted.

"What!"

"Let's call this stupid business off!" With the thaw, storm sewers would suck the teeth into Long Island Sound where they would change to pink and white flakes, mother of pearl.

But the jollies of that frozen evening weren't over by a long shot. As Sergeant Bill Wilson turned down my street, the squawkbox exploded with noise. "On my way," he said into the mike. Then, "This's started happening almost every night. But I've never been right on top of it." He ripped past my house without slowing.

"What?"

"Know Champion's Market?" he asked. "It's in your neighborhood."

"Sure."

"Cat Burglar just hit the place."

Gorgeous George's plate-glass front shone like a hearth, and I saw him pacing violently. Mrs. Champion, behind the counter, hid her face in her hands.

"Police," Sergeant Wilson said when we walked in.

"And Mrs. Shiflet-Biggs," said George, his voice shrunk in the wash. "Officer, is this the culprit?"

"Nonsense." Wilson's deer-hunter eyes looked about the

145

tiny store and seemed to focus on every object including the cigarette butts smashed against the floor. "What happened?"

"The notorious Cat Burglar," George said, "entered through a small basement window in the rear. We were awakened by his departure. Ah, has the local tabloid dispatched a man?"

"Oh, Mrs. Biggs," sobbed Mrs. Champion. "Who could have done such a terrible thing to Mr. Champion?" Her old pink robe looked all frayed, while George's curved his belly in a tidal wave of blue satin.

"Footprints in the snow," Wilson suddenly said. "There's a back door?" He collared George. They rushed behind the meat and disappeared.

"Poor Mrs. Champion." I hugged her. "You must feel awful." I could hear their children walking overhead.

"No Santa Claus this year."

"But you said the Cat Burglar."

Mrs. Champion nodded toward the counter, where a scrap of sackpaper lay. "But this time he was in luck," she sobbed, "and the Champions are out of it. That crook owes us so much!" She pointed to the floor beneath the cash register. A loose board had been lifted, opening a hole the size of a small strongbox. "Mr. Champion insists that if we tell the police all, we'll be in even deeper trouble."

Was there even one uncrooked soul in this world? I wondered.

"Dern Cat Burglar sure has his nerve," I said. It was the first poem I'd seen in the Cat Burglar's own childish lettering, done for camouflage:

> E'en in such cold, this doggerel pup
> Is on the verge of blowing up.
> An unloved waif, I freeze my moan,
> But feel the fire in my bone.
> Alive with rot, cause I got fucked,
> I'm homeless, Godless, out-of-lucked.
> So here I write, a puss ill fated
> To be so bad, and so vornated.
>
> Cat Burglar

"Christ," I said.

"Sounds as if the Cat Burglar has problems, too," Mrs. Champion said. "But why must the poor man use such language?"

"He's out of his crazy head," I told her. "That's why."

"And"—she looked down and blushed—"there's a filthy drawing on the other side. Would you . . . ?"

"Spare me," I said.

Wilson stormed back. George shuffled along behind. "Goddamn blizzard," Wilson said. "Well, I'll tell you one thing, he must've picked you tonight because he lives in the neighborhood. Not even that beanbrained bastard's going to travel far from home in this weather. So what'd he take?"

"Ah, I have not yet made a full and accurate tally," George said.

"You must have some idea."

"Ah, oh, one hundred dollars."

But I knew from George's eyes that Michael Silverspring, who at last, it seemed, had stuck Bess's word into a poem, had pilfered much more.

"Mrs. Shiflet-Biggs is holding the um latest example of his perfidious versifying."

I handed the scrap to Bill Wilson. "Brother," he said. "Idiot's doubled himself up into a dog. What's next, some rat? Fiery bone. Doesn't make sense."

"A dog and his bone," George offered. "Soup bone, perhaps."

"I doubt that," I said. "George, is there a bathroom down here?" remembering Michael's sickening bad aim.

"Mrs. Champion and I rush upstairs whenever nature calls," George said.

"What's this freeze-my-moan stuff, anyway?" Wilson asked. "Jeez, it's weird."

"The whole rhymes very cleverly," Mrs. Champion said. "It's not every burglar you need a dictionary to understand."

"For this moron?" Wilson cried.

"Vornated," I said.

"Like voracious?" Wilson said.

"Sir, poor grocer that I am," George said, "I happen to be

no slouch with words. If I may be so bold, no vornated inhabits the English tongue."

"Doesn't mean a thing," Sergeant Wilson said.

"That, sir—or it could mean anything," said George. "In my opinion, I have been thoroughly vornated indeed."

"Not to mention poor Ethel," I sighed, "who lies vornated in the arms of death."

"Did something befall your mother?" Mrs. Champion asked.

"Killed in a wreck," Wilson said.

"Poor dear!" Mrs. Champion embraced me. "And I was concerned with my own selfish cares. Here, take a little something for the children."

"*Woman!*" thundered George. "NO!"

But I was furious over that fool Michael robbing poor Mrs. Champion of her Christmas. What would he do, give the loot to his Savior, Wierwoo, the motorcycle freak? If the Cat Burglar was going to start robbing friends, I'd clip the bastard's whiskers. Or make him give fair exchange for what he'd stolen. Or something. As this night roared on, so many things got mixed up inside I couldn't tell the strip one landed from where another took off. "Have to ask Bess, at least, what vornated means," I thought out loud.

Placing the Cat Burglar's latest masterpiece in an envelope, Wilson asked, "Mrs. Biggs, do you know something else you're not telling me?"

"The poor woman has enough problems," Mrs. Champion scolded, "without mixing her up in ours."

"For heaven's sake, rush Mrs. Shiflet-Biggs home," agreed George. "Surely this woman is hindering your investigation. Off to bed with you. Get a job and pay me the balance of what you owe. Scat!"

"Us women have to look out for each other," Mrs. Champion said. "You men are bound and determined to pound us into the mud!" Whereupon she gave mountainous George such a glare he toppled backward a step.

"Somebody from the lab'll be over," Wilson told them, "soon as he can plow through these cruddy drifts."

148

I scooted onto the cold seat of Wilson's car, and in one corner of George's bright window, I suddenly noticed words—in crayon, maybe, or grease pencil. They looked like NO TRUST, printed backward. Good old Gorgeous George, I thought.

When we slid to a halt outside my house, I asked, "Hey, Bill, how many people you use that big gun on?"

"Not a proper subject," he replied.

"I'm curious. My daddy used to be a lawman, among a dozen other things. Ever win any medals for bravery?"

"Hoo boy," Wilson sighed. "Yep."

"Who'd you shoot for it?"

"Sixty mad dogs, busload of kids, fourteen little old ladies, like your father no doubt," he said. "Can I get back to work on those two cases that landed in my lap tonight?"

"*Two* cases?"

"The Cat Burglar," Wilson said. "That's one. And you. That's number two. Now, hop out. And don't let anything bust up your beauty rest."

"What the hell else are you trying to bug me with?" I yelled.

But he only drove off without another word, the S.O.B., leaving me to dangle all bothered, frustrated, and angry. I stomped into my house.

Marlene sat miserably on the floor, beside the blood-soaked couch. "Hi, Mamma," she said in a low voice. "Jenny told me about Grandma Dollarhide."

"Where's everybody?"

"Jenny and Bess are upstairs. When I got here, Errol Shiflet, Michael, and Joy Silverspring were in a three-way fight. Then the Silversprings split in different directions, and Errol took their screaming baby home. That left me alone with Grandma's awful boy friend. He sort of shuffled around making hideous gargling noises in his throat, like he was talking under water. Sounded like he said he was going to buy himself a bottle, dig a deep trench, and lie low."

"That's what Ethel's doing right now, lying low. She's dead, honey."

"I treated her pretty bad, didn't I?" Marlene said. "I'm sorry."

"How've you been, honey?"

"Oh, you know," Marlene said.

"But I don't." Marlene had always been so full of sass, this was the first time I could remember seeing her downright depressed. "Is it Grandma?"

"No."

"Something go sour between you and Jack?"

"What do you care?" Marlene pouted. "You forgot I was ever your daughter."

"Honey, you don't have to tell me anything." I sat and threw my arm over her shoulder. "I'm so confused I wouldn't be much help."

"Jack almost didn't let me go tonight," Marlene blurted. "He's known a long time I wanted to leave. He threatened to hurt me if I didn't come back." Then she was sobbing. I let her go till finally she got her voice. "Mamma, I'm scared of him."

"He seemed like a nice boy, Marlene. Ignorant, but good-hearted."

"He's a killer, Mamma."

"In a war," I said. "That's different."

"He told me exactly what he did," Marlene went on. "And, oh, Mamma, he showed me snapshots. He took them himself. You can't imagine—!"

"Now, Marlene. Some things you have to grow up to understand."

"No, that is not true." Marlene's voice grew sharp and clear. She looked me in the eyes. She told me, in detail, every lovely bit, the rapes, and not of women only, or even humans, the killings, and not in battle only, and not quick, and not only of adult men and women or even old people, as the atrocity pictures Jack Rader snapped made very clear to Marlene. What I had said out of my grown-up wisdom was not true. At all.

"Come up to your own bed, honey," I said. "We'll bolt the doors. I have a pistol. If Jack Rader breaks in, I'll—"

"Mother?" Marlene looked strange. "You would do that?"

"Yes," I said. "Your grandpa, my father, was a medic and saved lives during the war. At least that's what I heard. But right now I feel like a born killer."

That night I dreamed Bill Wilson broke down my door and, muttering, "Case," over and over, took me. After he spent himself, I groped Charlie's pistol from among the litter, the stone finger, the broken pencils, in the drawer next to my bed. And lifting Wilson's sleeping head by the hair from my bare breast, I shot him through the skull.

CHAPTER 19

Toothless and sunken-cheeked, Ethel rested in the cheapo pine coffin. Over her gleamed a big 3-D photo of Christ in lit-up Technicolor. A cord snaked from the frame behind the coffin. Michael Silverspring said the actor who posed looked like a respectable and holy Jesus. But Errol whispered loudly in my ear, "That male model was a roaring fag. Sucked the photographer's juices like a big queer spider."

"Errol, shut up," I said, thinking how my own photo had been plastered the evening before dead center on the newspaper's front page, Ethel in my lap, both of us washed in gore like a pair of bloody murderers.

Joy wasn't at the service, neither was Billy Graham. But Mrs. Champion, even though her store had been ripped off by the Cat Burglar, came out of pure sympathy. Marlene was there, minus Jack Rader at last. Bess kept badgering me to touch Grandma, and finally I let her. "Grandma feels cold like vanilla pudding," Bess said.

Jenny had come along the day before to pick out a coffin, and we'd both endured the young salesman's snottiness when I took the cheapest box in the house, a pine thing, disguised with phony gray felt. You could see dried glue at the seams. Earlier, I'd tried to find Billy, thinking he'd chip in something. But he had just plain vanished, as if into that icy cylinder of gas which was to be his grave. The head mor-

152

tician, a creep named Bales, demanded payment in advance. So once again I was flat broke.

When Michael Silverspring, who I fully considered the Cat Burglar, rose beside the coffin to read his Bible, I glanced around in time to see Sergeant Bill Wilson slip through the door, slide into the hindmost pew, and unscrew his Stetson. I felt sweat frosting my forehead.

"Dearly beloved, we are gathered here in the sight of God," Michael blabbed. I didn't realize till he'd run on a whole minute that the crazy fool was reading a marriage ceremony.

"O Lord," Errol whispered, stretching out his arms. "Drive in the nails!"

"It's because of you and Joy," I whispered back. "He wants to get in at least a small dig, after all the rooting around you've been doing."

Then it was time to bid Ethel goodbye. With Marlene, Jenny, and Bess beside me, I walked past Michael to the coffin. "So long, old gal," I said. "Hope you're less miserable now."

"Poor Grandmother," Jenny said sadly.

Bess said, "Pick me up, Mommy." Before I could stop her, Bess reached into the coffin again, grabbed one of Ethel's paws, and knocked it sideways.

Ethel's fingertips were black with ink.

"What was she doing?" Marlene whispered. "Digging her own grave?"

"Lord, I don't know!" I cried out. But once I'd had the same ink used on me, and now I felt my hands trembling beyond control.

"What's wrong?" Michael asked.

"Ethel must have been trying to bury something, like a cat," I said. "You know about cats, Michael."

"Cats?" Michael stared up at Jesus like an unworldly simpleton. "Cats have nine lives. Didn't the ancient Egyptians worship them as gods? Hum. Cats." I wondered if too many switches getting thrown at once hadn't caused a short circuit and burnt out his brain.

Mrs. Champion squeezed my hand. "It's terrible to lose a mother," she said. "Have yourself a good cry. It'll help."

Mr. Bales was here in person for some strange reason, since he'd been able to gouge so little for this shindig. A butterball the height and width of Mrs. Champion, he took hold of the coffin lid, already a little warped, and creaked it shut. Without the slightest warning, I began to bawl, watering Mrs. Champion's neck. Marlene and Jenny patted my heaving back. Some ray from outer space must have struck through the mortuary wall and fritzed a nerve. I couldn't stop for anything, the way little Axel must have felt since birth.

"There, darling," Mrs. Champion said. "It's all right."

I was no more in control than a driverless Mack truck hurtling down Everest. "Oh, sweet thing," she said. Pumping my brakes, I gradually pulled to a stop.

In one corner, Michael Silverspring stood biting his thumb. In another crouched Errol Shiflet shaking his big head. Bill Wilson wagged a thick finger down into the undertaker's face.

"Sergeant," I said, my sobs ironed out, "I'm glad to see you're looking out for an unfortunate woman."

"Cops aren't machines," Wilson said.

"Catch the Cat Burglar yet?" I glared angrily at Michael.

"Hot on his tail," Wilson said. "Ethel Peen's autopsy, by the way—"

Peen? I wondered, but didn't want to ask Wilson, where he got that name.

"Her abdomen was found to be one huge cancer. If it's any consolation for what you did, she'd have died anyway from internal and external bleeding."

We buried Ethel in the state's biggest and oldest graveyard, among crooked trees. A pee-yellow sun drizzled between the clouds, melting the snow to slush. My daughters stood with me there, so did Michael, Errol, and Mrs. Champion. While Michael abused his Bible to dig up the passage on ashes and dust, I saw a person wearing a long black coat, black shoes, and a wide-brimmed black hat walk between

154

the tombstones toward our neatly T-squared hole. Even the sun glasses were black, like a movie star's or a blind man's. He, she, or it stood smiling behind a stone cross twenty feet off.

"Who's that, Mommy?" Bess asked. "Is it Daddy?" Then she shot off to sniff the stranger out. I simply didn't have the strength to run after her.

"Some ghoul," Marlene said. "Probably saw that grisly picture of you and Grandma in the paper."

Michael started reading. The gravediggers lowered Ethel into the muddy ground. Jenny cried softly. Bess stayed talking to the stranger, who I hoped to hell was no pervert. When Michael's short service ended, the stranger promptly about-faced and walked away.

"Hope he got his jollies," Marlene said. "He looked familiar, but I don't know why."

"How can you even be sure it's a he," I asked, "in that outfit?"

Bess came back. "Not Daddy," she said.

"Who was it?" I asked.

"Mr. Lucky. He said 'Merry Christmas' to you, Mommy. He smelled like inside a closet."

"I don't know any Mr. Lucky," I said.

"He knows you, Mommy," said Bess. "He said, 'Tell your Mommy I knew her very well.' "

"Speaking of closets," Marlene said. "Something I found in *my* closet is pretty darned interesting."

After Michael dropped us off at home, Jenny walked Bess to the playground at Malcolm X, and Marlene led me upstairs to her room.

"Look in the closet," she said.

I looked. "Why, Ethel told me Billy had fenced these things!"

"Fenced," said Marlene. "Great."

Ethel's bag lay full of trinkets I'd swiped during my forays as fake Cat Burglar. Next to it flopped a large spiral notebook, my signature scrawled across its front. The inside looked like an inventory. An address I'd visited in the dead of the night headed each page, then a list of items. The handwriting was my own. It felt like those dreams where eating spinach and starting your car melt into lovemaking, for no reason except how the strings of your brain tie into a single gray knot.

And I suddenly knew that Ethel, master forger and counterfeiter, had eaten my food, slept in my house, and done her lying goddamndest to frame me with iron bars. That was why she'd carted in all that bogus money, in a pack now under my bed—not to bail me out of my misery, but to slam the prison door tight as a tomb. And not two hours before, I had bellowed over her death.

"What's been going on?" Marlene asked.

"Honey, I don't have the slightest idea."

"Don't, huh."

"Must be that junk she brought when she first came."

"But that's your handwriting."

I stared wide-eyed and innocent. "You know how Ethel was a world-champion forger."

"A decathlon winner in the crime field," Marlene groaned. "I sure prize my family history. Parachute me into the Women's Reformatory, I could win Queen of Thieves hands down."

That night I shredded the notebook and lugged the loot from Marlene's room to a closet in mine. Then I switched off my brain, blanketed the couch with old newspapers to shield me from Ethel's dried innards, and settled down to devour the *Elm City Journal*, which only the night before had featured me on its front page. I thought how each newspaper in Ethel's trash pile was chock-full of stories, terrible, funny, and sad, marriages, births, weather, murders, how many pounds of wool your average llama gives—and nobody could hope to sponge it all up, let alone decide how it hung together. You'd blow a fuse trying. For comfort, I thought of my Treasure House, like a happy childhood memory. There I could imagine objects in order, each in its rightful place, except for the newspaper, and those rubbers like slugs rotting on the oriental carpet. One of these days I'd return.

156

Women Christmas-shopping in downtown Elm City, I read, were getting robbed like mad at gunpoint, a real scandal. Had I locked my house tight? Because the Cat Burglar was flying as if by magic carpet from store to store. So numerous were the robberies, so thick the volume of poems, the cops hatched a theory that all sorts of false Cat Burglars were operating. I figured that loony Michael, who no more knew himself than a jellyfish, had given birth to disciples. The paper even found two new poems clean enough to print. One read:

> Is there no aspirin for my pain?
> Am I always chilled with rain?
> Must I wander sterile here
> Jammed and stuffed with frozen fear?
> Oh all who laugh in golden glee,
> You must end my misery!

"Golden glee" was Michael playing with his name, I figured. The rest was sheer nonsense, as if he'd trapped himself in a prison beyond just having to fire his rhymes straight. The second poem caused a sensation of sorts, and confirmed what I'd suspected all along, that the Cat Burglar mainly wanted to be caught because for some weird reason he wanted to be punished.

> On the night before Christmas
> As still as a mouse
> Just set out a Cat Trap
> And capture this louse.

This sounded like he intended to gift-wrap himself for the cops on Christmas Eve. So the newspaper announced it would begin a front-page countdown, saying each evening that only so many days remained till the Cat Burglar ripped off his mask to reveal his true identity.

And so that no run-of-the-litter crazy could claim the credit without deserving the fame, police announced they had been holding back three major clues from the newspapers—identifying clawmarks that only the true Cat Burglar would know and could name.

Next I hit a write-up about that wild rapist, disguised as a priest, who must have eaten Wheaties religiously. Lonzo would hang his head in shame. Heavily camouflaged and waving a pistol, Father Eleven Peter had raided a ladies' luncheon group. Afterward, he drank coffee and ate chicken salad like a guest speaker, helped the hysterical hostess clean up part of the mess, then shook the trembling hands of those poor housewives and left.

One line in the obits said Ethel Dollarhide was dead.

Halfway down the last page, I spotted an AP from Jasper, Indiana, concerning one Charles Roger Peen, 57. His eldest son, Billybob, 39, resident of the Indianapolis V.A. Hospital because he got paralyzed waist-down in Korea, grew flustered when his old man didn't answer the phone for three months, not even when the hospital tried to notify him that Billybob was about to croak from pneumonia. After recovering, Billybob phoned the Jasper fuzz and asked them to investigate.

I imagined the cold, musty smell that greeted the cops when they broke through Charlie's door and began digging for the chilly truth. They found it in the basement.

Electricity was running. Nosing around the furnace, one cop heard the humming motor of a padlocked deepfreeze. "Hey, big rods, come on down!" They crowbarred it open. Charlie Peen lay inside. Someone had emptied a small-bore automatic into his skull. Shell casings lay scattered about the basement, but police still sought the murder weapon. There was a small printing press in the basement as well, and a totally shattered plate, and police suspected that the murder was related to a counterfeiting ring long suspected of operating in the area.

Billybob showed the cops a letter his father had written the previous August, which led South Bend police to pick up a drifter, Buster Watson, 42. Cops nationwide had been alerted to hunt a second fugitive, name not released.

A retired printer who traded shots with Japs in World War II, Charles Roger Peen was survived by nineteen children, sired on roughly eleven different wives.

Junk crashed about my skull. Ethel's crap filled my house, tons of grime and slop all proving me guilty. The thaw had come, it seemed, and I grew frantic that Errol's Red Devil lay gasping on the soaked lawn, all that frenzy dying to a hunk of meat under the moon and stars. And Lonzo, in his cell—suddenly I knew I'd plunged him in deep trouble. I wanted to help, but felt paralyzed. I thought of Jack Rader, as if I myself had committed his atrocities. I had to do something, but my numb bones wouldn't stir. What would happen to Jenny, to Bess? Already my bad luck had ruined their lives. A terrible chill flowed around my heart. Poor Becky Willett, what had become of her? I had blasted Charlie Peen, stuffed him in the deepfreeze. I had busted the limestone Joe Palooka, robbed the Champions of their Christmas, burned Errol with clap, cut his throat. I disemboweled Molly Fiddler and drove Michael Silverspring mad. Lord, I thought, I've got to stop this! But how could I haul that crud from my house before it sprang to life in one snotty glob? Thanksgiving had passed my family by, and now Christmas chugged down like a steam engine, me lashed to the tracks and no hero to hack my knots. I had trusted all to Ethel, who lay dumb in the icy ground. One hope whispered, a crackly long-distance voice in my brain, that the Salvation Army would relieve me of all rotting junk. But it was too late at night. Their trucks were locked, engines a deepfreeze. Frost hardened my veins as sleep slammed down like a trap door made of ice.

CHAPTER **20**

I'm a tough bird to keep grounded, or I'd have crashed head first into the loony bin long ago. Next morning I awoke fired to do something, though I wasn't sure just what. Knocked flat by some virus, which made me wonder if that stranger in the graveyard wasn't diseased, Bess still slept in her room.

Then Errol pecked at the kitchen door. Sheepish and shuffling like those black Hollywood actors before Malcolm X put his foot down, he held his cup out to borrow sugar.

"Come in, take the load off," I said. "How's life with the Silversprings?"

"I'm their nigger," Errol said. "Pardon the term, because I'm a staunch supporter of civil rights. They've got me doing their cooking and cleaning. Rest of the time, I babysit Axel. Amelia, I thought you were the world's champion ball-cutter. Let me apologize. Joy doesn't even have a worthy second. In some crazy way, I think she wants me around mainly because of you. I'm just a stand-in, so to speak."

"Get away from her," I said, "while you have a chance."

"I'll act out my degradation to the bitter end," said Errol. "No wonder that little bastard Axel howls most of the time."

"Just letting out his feelings," I said. "We'd be better off if we all did."

In my clingy nightgown, I caught Errol eyeballing me hard. "You're getting fat," he said.

"Pregnant."

"Jesus H. Christ." He looked more down-and-out than usual. "Who stuck it to you this time?"

"None of your business."

"Did he give you that stupid green ring for letting him put it to you all night?"

"Sew your filthy mouth shut. I wasn't responsible."

"Lord, who *is*, in this fucked-up world? Merry Christmas, Amelia."

"Merry Christmas, Errol." I watched him shuffle back to God knows what.

But he reminded me that I ought to hustle my girls' Christmas, and it'd be handier if I had a car. In last night's paper, the one that so flummoxed me, I searched the classified till I read, "1960 Rambler," called, of all things, "Godzilla." They wanted $80.

I tried mining my dingy bedroom for money—looked under my mattress, in the nightstand drawer, in old shoes, in knotted nylons. Nothing. Not a cent. Finally I decided, what the hell, what could I possibly lose now?

When I called the number, a girl answered. "I want Godzilla," I said.

"How much you want to pay, lady?"

"If you handle plate and title transfer, a hundred."

"Lemme ask my fren." Muffled sounds. "Okay." Another pause. "How come you be buyin a eighty-dollar car, lady?"

"Don't ask me why I do things."

"Well, we be sellin Godzilla to eat. And I don't want no damn check."

"I'll pay you," I said, "with a crisp hundred-dollar bill."

I finished dressing seconds before Godzilla mushed up outside, the second ugliest car I ever saw, second to Casey's junk heap. It looked like an un-Sanforized Continental, shrunk to fit a dwarf whose legs had been sawed off. I fell in love at once. It had two doors. The paint was flat black rind on steel, sponging in all light. Life seemed to stop in its tracks.

Then out climbed the most gorgeous girl, equal to Marlene.

Bess banged unsteadily downstairs. "Who's there, Mommy?" I opened the door with Bess hugging my thighs.

Tall and lean, the girl wore an orange coat that barely covered her privates. I wondered if she even had a dress on. "Drive round the block," she said, "if it suit your taste."

"Mommy!" Bess cried. "She has yellow eyes!"

"Watch out," said the girl. "I ain't takin nobody's shit."

"No swearing in my house," Bess said.

"Don't jive me, child!" the girl shot back.

"That's a great big black girl," Bess said.

"Bet your tail," said the girl. "Your daddy needs to lift up your little dress and give it a big whack."

"Does she mean my bottom, Mommy?" Bess asked.

"Lord, I don't know."

"You smell good," Bess said.

The girl stopped scowling and grinned.

"Let's get down to business," I said. "Suddenly I don't feel too damn red hot." I was dizzy, and my mouth felt cottony. I reached into my purse, and the girl's eyes looked like they would explode. Without thinking, I had pulled out the whole thick green loaf of Ethel's fake dough.

"My God," murmured the girl. "You ain't jivin."

I peeled off a portrait of randy Ben, father of many bastards. The paper felt real enough. Handing it to the girl, I held my breath, but she couldn't stop gaping at the wad in my hand.

So for the hell of it, I gave her another phony bill, that looked as real as it felt. "Transfer and plates, remember?" I said. "And fast. I want to hit Macy's tonight and get Christmas for my kids."

Finally the girl told Bess, "Lucky kid, you must got a rich daddy."

"Rich, ha," I said. "We're dirt-poor."

"Lady, you don't make no sense," said the girl.

An hour later, when she came back, she said, "Hope Macy's got what you need."

"So do I," I said.

That night after dinner I grabbed my purse and drove

162

downtown, not half sure what I was really up to. Either I had Bess's virus or Errol had transferred his clap to me through the air. The stop light where Ethel died held me so long I almost ran through. Then I had to wind round a ramp in the huge parking garage attached to Macy's, cars like kernels of corn, till finally I surfaced on top, wind blowing like ice. On the way up, I'd passed a half dozen cops, but here, except for two other cars, I was alone. I wondered if maybe I could be arrested for not paying Macy's anything on all those goods I charged. The duns kept growing more and more vicious.

An army jammed the store, elbowing around like Vikings. The mob waiting to crush Santa's lap snaked two hundred feet, blocking aisles, and I remembered reading how back home in Indiana one father had knifed another for elbowing into line. Doing a soft-shoe in the lingerie section, I finally heard the Muzak that danced me around like Pinocchio. This so bugged me that I pitched an armload of panties onto the carpet. My fellow shoppers were knocking cosmetics and toys haywire, misplacing best sellers among kids' watches. It could be a regular jamboree for shoplifters.

The longer I shoved through the crowd, the angrier I grew. Five-and-dime candy smell jittered my nerves like ether at Dr. Burke's. I didn't have one gift in mind and couldn't see any junk worth buying or even stealing, and the next person who elbowed me was going to get creamed. So I fought to an elevator and elbowed myself inside. Of course it stopped at every floor.

At the top, two others remained. "Les hep the lady."

"Why yes. Ladies fuhs." They moved to each side, nodding and smiling, holding the doors so I could saunter through.

Wind cooled my temper as I walked to Godzilla, now the only heap on that concrete field. When I reached for the car door, an arm hooked past mine. "Jus let me do that, ma'am. You be tired after foolin roun in there so long."

"Thas right." The other man walked around the car.

Wind filled my ears. "Why, thank you." Shuddering violently, I sank behind the wheel.

An icy gun muzzle pressed my nose. "You money or you life."

The other scooted onto the seat beside me whispering, "We gon fuck you ass, bitch." He yanked the purse off my lap. His switchblade gleamed. "We gon slice off you head." A hot blast of wine.

The gunman squeezed into the back seat. "Drive this mothuhfuck!"

"I'm pregnant," I whispered.

"Ain't no baby gon save you, bitch," said the switchblade.

"Baby gon feel my dick," hissed the man in back, with the gun. "Staht up!"

The other dug his knife into my purse. "Mothuh! She was fuckin straight!" With his free hand, he lifted the fat green wad.

"Shee-it!" The gunman grabbed wildly—and caught a handful of blade. Blood flew all over the car. "Fuckuh!" He leveled the pistol between his partner's eyes.

"Be cool," the other pleaded. "Plenty here. Les go now, my fren."

"Yes!" I shouted. "Scram!"

They scrambled for the stairs. Cold tickled my bottom where I'd peed myself.

After a few minutes another face peered in. "All right, lady?"

"I was *robbed!*" I yelled.

"Two men?"

"Yes. Black."

"What shade?" the cop asked. "Dark, medium, light."

"Ah, dark," I said.

"Dark, like me?" the cop asked.

"Yes!" I cried, in gratitude.

"I'm medium," the cop said.

He yanked a radio off his belt and spoke softly. A voice crackled back.

"Going to the station, lady," he said. "Lock your car. We already caught your men next level down, guy with his knife still out, other with a revolver, and a bloody hand. Looks like they robbed a bank."

When I climbed out, my soaked coat was already freezing solid. Passing a phone booth, I had a sudden memory through my fear and dizziness. "Hey, officer. Got a dime?" I asked.

He dug in his blue pants. "Make it quick."

I rummaged my gutted purse for the prescription sheet. Nobody answered the first number, his office probably. At the second number, a sleepy voice said, "Ball."

"Hi there. I'm Amelia Biggs."

Sergeant Wilson led me to a basement stinking of tobacco, spit, and pee. As I staggered into a room, dark but for the bright stage, Bill Wilson waved a mutilated hand. Men paraded on stage, and I saw the pair who attacked me. "Pick them out," said Wilson, with a big, satisfied grin.

"Who?" I said.

"The men— Who what?"

"I don't see one familiar soul."

"By Jesus," groaned Wilson, "I think this old man's ulcer just sprung a leak. Mike!"

A man down front said, "You two, move!"

"Yah, pig," one of them grunted.

"They look like villains," I said, as the guilty men stepped forward and squinted into the footlights.

"Identify them," Wilson said.

"Who?" I said.

"Goddamn it!" Wilson shouted. "You boys better confess. We got her right here."

"Shee-it, pig."

"Fuck you, pig."

"We'll waste you with murder one. You grabbed that stuff tonight. Or you ripped it off two days ago in Bridgeport when you cut an eighty-year-old woman in her bed!"

"Pig, you know we ain't—"

"We got you for possession of illegal, stolen weapons. Resisting arrest. Suspicion of rape, robbery, and counterfeiting. You're nailed already on vagrancy, dope, public intoxication, prison escape, being suspicious persons, and foul and abusive language to a police officer. Hell no, nice boys like you wouldn't *kill* anybody!"

"We didn't do nothin, pee-ig."

"Yes." Wilson clacked his teeth. "Fine. Mrs. Biggs, *move!*"

Upstairs, he ordered me to sit, jerked open a desk drawer, and pulled out Ethel's wad. "Where did you come by almost fifty thousand phony bucks?" But for the worthless money, and a large manilla envelope, his desk was bare.

"Is my name on the bills," I said, "like Ivy Baker Priest?"

"No, goddamn it! But Ethel Peen's might as well be!" He pounded the desk. "Mrs. Biggs, this is yours! They stole it from you. They *had* to!" He paused. Then, trying his damnedest to force a smile, he held the money toward me. "They're good," he said. "Real good. You could've fooled me. If all the goddamn serial numbers weren't the same."

"No." I felt wildly strange, glad to be rid of it. I wouldn't take that fake green even if it was real and I could wing out free. "Give it to the poor," I told him.

"If I want to hold you, I will hold you!"

I managed to smile.

"In jail!" he snapped. "Tell me where this crap came from."

"Worrying the same old bone," I said.

"Okay, dollbaby. Let's get back to Ethel. We shot her prints through the Washington computer. Arrest record five blocks long."

"Mamma," I sighed. "You fingerprinted her when she was dead in her coffin, you dirty bastard."

"Bastard?" he chuckled and from the envelope on his desk yanked several documents. "The woman you buried is a forger, counterfeiter, and murderess. Ethel Peen."

"Poor old Mamma."

He settled his chin in the palm of his big, maimed hand.

166

"Speaking of bastards, who *was* your mamma?" he asked.

I started to say something flip, then kept still, mouth gaping like a daughter of Lot.

"Got a marriage license here," Wilson said. "A birth certificate. Adoption papers. Miss Dollarhide, I doubt if anybody now knows who your real mother was. But she was *not* Ethel Peen."

Ball came in as Wilson was saying, "A Casey Dollarhide appears to have fathered you, though even that isn't perfectly clear. Ethel ah Dollarhide then took you on apparently after some other slut of his gave birth." He held out some pieces of paper. "Want to look?"

"No," I murmured.

"All this was right on file, because your mother or whatever the hell you want to call her once beat a rap by proving she was real loving and charitable. Adopted a poor little orphan—you. Want my opinion, both your so-called parents were fake to the bone."

"Have you told Mrs. Biggs her rights?" Ball asked then. He was plump and cute, though he reminded me of a penguin. "Do you know this woman is pregnant?" His mustache flapped when he talked.

I was laughing, I couldn't put on my brakes.

"Hi, Bobby," said Wilson. "Situation normal, all fucked up. We were pouring gas on Mrs. Biggs' family tree."

"Your usual crummy shock tactics," Ball said. "This woman's hysterical."

"Junior, don't bug me till you get potty-trained," Wilson said.

"Ah ha ha ha ha haaaah!"

I grew aware that both men were patting my shoulders at the same time. Finally Ball said, "I'll need help getting her home. I don't drive."

"Good God, son," groaned Wilson. "Let me sign your beginner's permit, when you work up enough nerve."

"Here's where we stand," my lawyer shot back. "You

cops brutally harassed this pregnant woman after an accident killed her mother. Did you file charges? No. Was she guilty of anything? No."

"Mother, ha," Wilson said.

"Now you're brutalizing her because she's been most viciously robbed. Are you filing charges against her now?"

"No," Wilson said.

"Then where's your decency? Just where the hell is it?"

"Ahhhhhh." I settled into numbness. "Take me to Godzilla."

They dropped me off on the windy concrete slab.

"Hey, junior," said Wilson, "let's light somewhere for a drink, if you've reached legal age."

"Love a few," my lawyer said. "Don't have a damn thing else going for me tonight."

But I did—a yellow skating rink on my car seat. And then a nightmare bedful of hairy goblins, horny and energetic, scrambling over my skin like I had D.T.s. I lost track of the days. Whenever I stumbled into the trash heap of my home, children scattered like birds before a shotgun. Once I came to in the living room, match aflame in my hand inches from a newspaper that proclaimed, FIVE DAYS TILL CAT BURGLAR ZERO HOUR.

Another time on a cold street corner, I realized that I stood hectoring a squat old woman, total stranger, who looked a tiny bit like Ethel. "Get lost," the woman said. "Or I'll scream."

I was a monster from the depths. The National Guard would clank down the streets of Elm City to do me in. Pierce me with a sliver of the shack where I was raised, shoot me with a squirtgun filled at the L, and I would shrivel like Superman nailed with Kryptonite.

It seemed like I sleepwalked for days. Then one night I found myself edging Godzilla through snow before my Treasure House. The moon, nearing full, burned the sky clear. There must have been a second blizzard, the snow lay so deep. I had been aware, driving out, that a car behind me had spun off the road, after I'd slid safely across a patch of ice. I staggered through waist-deep drifts up my memory of steps, then reached through a broken pane.

Sheltered by darkness, I dug in my coat pocket and among the lint felt a book of matches. Something was wrong, like once when I was a child awake in the dark, and beside my pallet lay a monster, all warts and flippers, patient as a snapping turtle in the muck. I had been so wounded by terror I couldn't move when it stifled me with its clammy weight.

I struck a match, and it was as if every memory I had was a false one, like a glossy painting disguising a can of vile slime.

Had Ethel's curse landed here, too? Trash filled the living room. Something had sledgehammered the organ, whacked the pipes all crooked, knocked the keyboard's teeth out. But looking closer, I saw that it wasn't a real organ at all—only a wood and plaster prop, put there for interior decoration. Woodcarving on the walls had also been splintered, except for a child's face, eyes flicking over me. And I saw that all this carving, too, was fake, plaster of Paris poured into a mold and painted to look like wood. Was my poem still under all that junk? Fire bit my fingers and died.

In the hall, I lit a second match. The library had been shredded, heaps of paper and binding, bookshelves crushed to kindling. Only the sun porch, a mess to start, seemed as before. Vandals had let the windows be; shattered glass might have fought back. Under another flickering match, the newspaper lay where it had lain. I saw John Kennedy washed by ocean, before the match ate my fingertips and I dropped it and moved on.

From the basement rose a stench, sweet, rotten, and awful, a throat full of decayed flesh, like the breath that once hit me from Billy Graham's mouth. Something now breathed, low and sad, wind across a swamp, "Ahhhh!" as if a voice called my name. Hell glowed behind me.

And I stepped backward into the mouth of light, of monstrous heat. Sparks and shadows raced like schools of fish. Glass snapped, bones in the mouth of some beast. Blasts

169

of air cried from everywhere. A great wind booted me suddenly through an open window and I crashed into banked snow on the porch and staggered to my car.

The Sound was on fire, a tongue of white flame licking across the water at the moon's track. I forced myself to look around. Where the house had been stood a fiery skyscraper sighing like a lover. Waterfalls gushed from the porch. My tires grabbed pavement, and I took off.

My house stood dark. Fumbling for the lock, I found the front door ajar. Carefully I skirted the junk, whose position I now knew perfectly in the dark. But at the foot of the stairs, I tripped over a strange bundle and wondered if Marlene and Jenny were cleaning house. High time. In my bedroom, I stubbed my toe on the big conch.

I undressed. The dark room smelled strange, like somebody needing a bath. Slowly, as my eyes adjusted, a form rose from my mattress. The greasy automatic lay in my nightstand drawer clear on the other side of the bed. I wanted to yell, but feared this creature might rape and murder my girls, too, if they woke and rushed in. So I teetered naked and trembling, about to faint away.

"Amelia, that you?"

"Oh, Lord Jesus, yes."

"Merry Christmas," said Lonzo Biggs.

CHAPTER *21*

"Don't turn on the light!" we both whispered at once.

"You dern fool," I said. "My hair's gone white. How'd you get here?"

"Easy, honey," Lonzo said. "Ain't enough left of me to grease your soles, thanks to you."

"Isn't that the way," I shot back. "Show me a man who's made his life a torn-down mess, I'll show you someone who blames a woman."

"Don't want no fight," Lonzo said.

"If you think I'm to blame, how come you're here? To get even?"

"Ain't no place to hide," he said.

"How come you broke out? Those letters you wrote, I thought the warden's wife and daughter were wrapped round your—"

"I'm a dumbass," said the dark form on my mattress, "and them letters was stupid. And I ain't interested in gettin even with nobody no more. I done got so even I'm ahead. Lord, Amelia, take pity. I done been punished enough."

He sounded so beat, so down and out. "What is it, Lonzo?" I asked.

"Never should of badgered you into writing me," he said. "Didn't you know they read what comes in and goes out? How come you went and added that P.S.?"

"P.S.?"

"Where you wondered had I got into the pants of the warden's wife, who'd smuggled out my letter. Oh, Amelia, five minutes after the warden read that P.S., I was drug to Wing Nine where they cage the queers. They throwed me into the showers with three huge black fairies. And what went on is too pitiful to describe."

"What you feared the most," I murmured.

"After them guys done me in, I got stuck with this fairy cellmate built like Superman. Couldn't of protected myself with a elephant gun." Lonzo fell silent awhile. "Compared with this bozo," he went on, "I wasn't but a cocksucking flea." He paused. "Guess you sort of saved me after all, though, cause if it wasn't for your letter, I never would of had to break out. Made this plan, cause it was Christmas, and I heard that's the best time to make a break."

"How come?"

"Christmas time, them pigs that run the slammer sort of relax and goof off, and a lot are away with their families. So last time Superman made me a queer," Lonzo said, slowly grinding his teeth, "I give the faggot a special present. Planned ahead, like when we done stole things together, you and me. Killed him the only way I could. But before he keeled over for running out of blood, he wiped the cell up with my body. So they sticked me in the hospital, like I figured. Them two guards thought I was worse off than I really was and got blind drunk on Christmas spirits. Midnight yesterday, I split a couple heads, stole a guard's uniform and overcoat, and by Jesus I done walked out past the Christmas tree. Couldn't of managed it any other time of year. Hot-wired a couple of cars. Hitched a ride. And here I am."

"You killed a con?" I said, terrified but sort of proud, too. "And two guards?"

"Don't care a dry turd."

"But this is the first place they'll look."

"Probly," said Lonzo in a dead voice.

"You've got to go. What about our girls?"

"Only two's mine," Lonzo said. "You got one off that faggot Shiflet."

"You wouldn't harm the one in my belly." I'd flopped it out before I thought.

"That the big problem with your body you mentioned before the P.S.? They finally give me your letter in Wing Nine . . . Well, lemme feel," Lonzo said.

"Get your murdering hands off." But they already lay on me, one big palm holding my bottom, while the other roughed my belly.

"While I was getting queered upside down in the pen," Lonzo said, "you done been out fucking up a storm."

"No I have not. And what about the six-year-old you rolled in the rack? Pull your paws off my skin."

"Wasn't no six-year-old." But his hands dropped. Even in the dark I saw his big shoulders wilt. "Forgive me. I ain't myself, though probly that ain't no great loss."

The old funlover did have his good points. What he'd told me was awful enough for anybody to go through, but especially when it sapped juice from a man who so enjoyed life, though at other people's expense. "Aw, Lonzo, you've been through a pretty rough spell." I patted his head. "We've already taken the worst each other could dish out."

"Always sent the alimony when I could. Didn't have to."

"I know, Lonzo."

"Lord, I'll take off now. Got so tard, I needed a place to flop till I caught my breath. Honey—"

"What, Lonzo?"

"Come lie a minute."

I'd melted enough that though he smelled kind of gamy, I flopped right down. We hugged bare naked. Then I told him, "Go ahead, if it'll make you feel better."

Lonzo tried awhile, but got nowhere. "Can't," he said. "Too far gone, wore out and bunged up."

I remembered the limestone finger he'd given me so many years ago for luck, and Ethel's last sack of loot in my closet. "Lonzo," I said, "if you can't take any off me, I do have a couple things for when you go."

I climbed from the bed. Without turning on a light, I opened the drawer, lifted out the limestone finger and the tiny pistol. Moving to the closet, I hauled out Ethel's bag. Then from curiosity I hooked back the pistol's hammer till it caught.

"What's that noise?" Lonzo asked.

"Mistake," I mumbled. I had no idea how to release the hammer without shooting. So I bent to the conch and shoved the cocked pistol inside. "Get dressed, Lonzo. Here's some stuff you can pawn. Take my car."

"Aw, honey, keep your things. They'll catch me, you know that. Then they'll poach me like a egg."

"Take this," I insisted. Duds scraped his flesh. "Girls know you're here?"

"Come in real quiet. But that ornery Ethel sleeps light, don't she?"

"Ethel died," I said.

"Bull." He was tying his shoes. "That rip's gonna hang round forever."

"Dead," I repeated. "Six feet deep."

"Lordy Lord." Lonzo had dressed. "Luckier'n me, for dang sure. What's this here rock?"

"Joe Palooka's finger. For luck."

"Kept it all these years. Amelia, if I wish a thing, it's that I'd of treated you better. Now hang a robe on that pretty figger and see me out."

I thrust the gunnysack and car keys into his hands. "Pawn the things out of state," I said. I slid my blue robe on and padded barefoot behind him down the dark hall.

At the front door, I kissed his cheek. "Good luck, honey."

"Need it bad," said Lonzo. And he slipped out so fast I never had a chance to see his face.

"Who was that one, Mamma?" Marlene had come down noiselessly.

Yelling started outside. Marlene rushed round me and threw open the door.

174

"I done forced her!" Lonzo shouted.

"Freeze!"

"Daddy?" Marlene asked.

"Lookit this gunnysack, Bill!"

"Them's mine!" cried Lonzo.

I raced out on the porch beside Marlene. Cold air blasted my front.

Lit by moonlight, a ragged figure ran round Godzilla toward the sidewalk. Bill Wilson hollered, "That's it, you bastard!" and shot his huge gun three times at the figure's back, flinging him splat against a huge oak.

A cop in uniform rushed to look. Marlene bit her knuckles and whined. Wilson stood in the street behind my car, his cold eyes freezing me, and I realized that my robe was open, and I stood naked to zero weather. "Let's get in the house," I said.

"That was Daddy," Marlene sobbed.

Wilson stormed the porch, gun in one hand, paper flapping in the other. "Cover yourself, woman, for God's sake. Inside! This is a search warrant." Two patrol cars hissed to a stop at my curb. Cops with crowbars poured out. I heard an ambulance wail.

"Guy's dead as shit!" someone shouted.

My door slammed shut.

"You're under suspicion for harboring two murderers," Wilson said. "God knows what other charges we'll have after we rip your house to pieces."

"Pig!" Marlene shouted. "You murdered my dad!"

"He murdered three men yesterday, kid— Hey! Stop that! You guys, hold her *back!* Now let's take this joint apart!"

Cops went into action by slitting the fat couch where Ethel had started bleeding to death. When they smashed into the walls, I felt their crowbars in my guts. Plaster shattered over the messy rooms of my mind.

Bess crying in my arms, I wandered through the blizzard of dust and splinters to the kitchen, where I found Sergeant Bill Wilson gasping hard beside the dark hole in the wall, crowbar rigid in his hand. "You shot him because you were jealous," I said.

He only glared, then plunged back into demolition. White with plaster, Jenny sat like a zombie in the dining room. One deadly piece of evidence remained, hermit crab deep in its shell where those dummies never thought to hunt.

CHAPTER 22

Surrounded by a dust cloud, Bill Wilson and his home-wrecking crew led me a last visit to the station house. Third time's the charm. One other culprit occupied the large room, a young man who looked like that long-dead actor James Dean, handcuffed to a chair. I wore Marlene's galoshes, and over my robe the coat I charged at Macy's and never paid for. The young man wore a black topcoat, black eye, and split lips curled into a shocked grin. Two angry fuzz cracked fingers like bullwhips before his face—and suddenly he waved, as if he had once known me well.

As Wilson pointed me to the chair beside his desk, Father Time hobbled through the door. "Sergeant William Wilson," he creaked.

"Here."

"Western Union."

Wilson tore into the yellow envelope. "Let your shift," he muttered, reading. "Where the hole . . . Jesus." Half grinning, half scowling, he said, "Amelia Dollarhide Biggs Shiflet Biggs, what planet did you spin off of? Surely not Mother Earth." He stuffed the telegram into a pocket. "Okay, down to business."

Whether Ball would show depended on whether Michael, Joy, or Errol had called him.

Around 3 A.M., Wilson had hollered, "We're going downtown!"

Not having the heart to leave my girls in the wreckage of their home, let alone hauling them to the clink with me, I had sat on my slashed mattress and dialed the Silversprings.

"God love you," Michael answered, above the trumpeting yowls of Axel.

"Errol there?"

"Joy!" he shouted. "Errol sacked out with you?" Muffled yells. "He's coming," Michael said.

"Tell him to rush."

"I don't know," Michael whispered. "Lately Joy's acting crazy as a loon. What—"

"Who wants Errol?" Joy snapped into the phone.

"His ex-wife," I said.

"Hi, Amelia. How're tricks?"

"Can I send my girls over?"

"The whole brothel?" said Joy. "I've got some important plans for tonight. After all, it's Christmas."

"Sergeant Wilson's tearing my house apart with crowbars and sledgehammers. When they finish, they're hauling me to jail."

"Are you guilty of stealing money, honey? Have they found evidence of anything?"

"No," I said. "And they aren't going to."

"Then you'll be back home later?"

"If there's any justice in the world."

"Then maybe I'll stop by and leave a little Christmas surprise," Joy said. "Send your girls over now. And call me when you're coming home. Here's Errol."

"Ungh."

"I'm sending the girls there," I said. "Call my lawyer for me."

"Good lay?" Errol asked.

I told him about Lonzo and Sergeant Bill Wilson. Then I gave him Ball's phone numbers.

Errol paused. "The Prince of Peace was born today," he said. "And I feel like killing somebody."

Now, in the big pee-smelling room, Sergeant Wilson said, "Burn down any houses tonight?"

"You sure ripped mine apart," I said.

"I've had you followed ever since you wouldn't identify those characters who stole your counterfeit hundred-dollar bills. What's wrong, Mrs. Biggs?"

Finally I said, "If you had some yahoo spying on me, you might as well quit playing cat and mouse."

"Cat and mouse." He cracked his knobby knuckles. He looked at the glossy top of his desk.

And I remembered the car behind me that had spun out on the ice. Had its driver watched helplessly when a house blew up in the direction we'd both been heading?

Then up bounced William Robert Ball, Jr. "If you hauled this woman here to harass her again," he started. But he was still too sleep-stunned to find a proper threat.

"Woman? You mean this psychopath? She belongs in a freak show."

"The night this cop took you for a drink," I told Ball, "it was so he could have me tailed in peace."

Wilson blinked.

"I've never been so miserable and flustered in my life," I went on. "They let poor Lonzo go into my house, then waited in ambush till he came back out. So they could murder him."

"Nonsense," Wilson said, looking a little sheepish.

"Then what is the sense?" asked Ball.

"We knew Biggs'd broken prison and murdered to do it. But that's all we knew, except that he might be dumb enough to contact this psycho here. When our tail"—he paused, looked me in the face, and scowled—"radioed he'd lost her, we immediately staked out her house. Biggs just happened to be inside already. When he ran off that porch, it knocked us for a loop."

"Knocked Lonzo for a bigger one, you bastard," I said. "And how come you already had a search warrant?"

"Search warrant?" Ball perked up. "What search warrant?"

Wilson shook his big wooly head. "Mrs. Biggs, for a woman who's so flustered, you do land on your feet. Not to mention your brilliant telegram."

"What telegram?" asked Ball.

"It's my trump card," Wilson said.

"All right, Bill, then let's see that so-called search warrant." Ball had blown wide awake. "Because I can't imagine the grounds on which all of a sudden you managed to get one granted."

"Mrs. Biggs saw it, didn't you, Mrs. Biggs?"

He was bluffing. I could scarcely believe my luck. "All I saw was a piece of paper flapping in my face," I said. "For all I know it was a pinup of somebody else you murdered."

"You didn't have a search warrant," Ball said flatly. "You were just desperate."

"Look, every cop in the country's on the alert for that character and he comes out of her house. Plus her mother. I mean, Amelia Biggs's a magnet for every felon in the United States!"

"You were gambling," Ball said. "Now you're going to need fifty-two trumps to blunder out of this snafu. I've never seen such confused, incompetent, illegal police work in my whole professional life."

"All five minutes of it," Wilson said.

"Precisely what evidence did you wreck her home to find?"

"Jesus save me," said Wilson, hiding his face in his big hand, unable to answer.

"You murdered this pregnant woman's husband before the eyes of his children on Christmas Eve, tore her home to shreds on a gamble, and found no evidence of anything!"

"Biggs had it with him," muttered Wilson.

"Prove that!" I fired back. "Lonzo yelled it was all his, and then you shot him dead. Marlene heard it all. What's more"—I lifted my voice to a cry—"Wilson murdered Lonzo out of sheer jealousy!"

"By Jesus, woman," shouted a purple Wilson, "I have never faced a more hardened criminal!"

"Slander!" Ball cried. "We'll sue. You're a desperate man."

"Yeah," Wilson said grimly. "And I may damn well do something even more desperate before this insanity ends."

The young man in the black topcoat, and his two interrogators, had been staring silently at us. "Hello there, Amelia," he called. "I know you."

"The whole damned United States," groaned Wilson. "That's just what I said."

"You do?" I asked the stranger.

"Father confessor!" the gleeful young man said. "Think back over your life with Ma Bell."

"Do you know a nice girl named Becky Willett?" I wondered if, at last, I was seeing the Cat Burglar, in the flesh. This character was screwball enough for sure.

"Jesu Christe, I don't remember half the bodies I plumbed, especially the last few days. I've been staggered by an ungodly virus. But, dear lady, I remember *your* body." He bunched fingertips at his mouth, "Pah!" then made an open flower of his hand. "And, more abstractly, your mother's as well. Remember the onlooker at her burial?"

Dazed and flummoxed, I was figuring him out.

"Who is this joker?" Sweat washed Wilson's meaty face.

"A wicked knave, Father," the young man said. "A great stealer of tarts."

"Folks, meet Brother DeProspo," a cop said. "He hides in that monastery beside Malcolm X, when he's not on the prowl."

"The ecumenical spirit in action," Brother DeProspo said.

"Chief himself caught the good monk attacking the chief's old lady under their Christmas tree tonight."

"Decided to follow the Cat Burglar's lead and make it a grand slam," Brother DeProspo said. "And you, child"— though I had ten years on him, at least—"have you paid for our wet sin together?"

"It's drawing interest." My palm trembled against my tummy. "Here." Brain almost bursting, I knew at last the blind prick who screwed me awake that black September night. "And you're a *father?*" I cried.

"An *expectant* father!"

"Would anybody report me if I drilled this jerk between the eyes?" Wilson asked.

"I'll send for the Pope's blessing," the young rapist told me.

"I'm no snapper," I shot back. "Tell Pope Whosit to stick it! That was a terrible thing you did, Father, and I don't forgive you a bit!"

"Neither does the poor chief," a fuzz said. "Not to mention his wife. She's in the hospital, suffering from shock. And they've got the chief on knockout drops to keep him from killing this joker himself."

"There I was, my children," Brother DeProspo said, "nailed to the cross."

"Haw haw!" laughed the cops.

"Wilson," Ball said, "I'm going to nail you. Release this woman. Stop all harassment. Next time you want some kicks, take in Clint Eastwood."

"Whenever they resurrect him, I recommend James Dean," Brother DeProspo cut in. "*East of Eden,* where he faces the beast of his past. *Rebel Without a Cause,* where he confronts his monster psyche."

"Are you the Cat Burglar, too?" I asked.

"As you well know," said Sergeant Wilson, reaching into the pocket where he'd shoved the telegram, "this lunatic is *not* the Cat Burglar."

Did he know something about Michael? I wondered.

"My double, my brother! We march to the same mad drummer," Brother DeProspo leered, licking his split lips. "Chaos and old night. Has he given himself up tonight like he promised? I'm dying to meet whoever showed me the way to freedom."

"Son of a bitch." Wilson rolled his eyes. "James Dean," he finally announced, "was a raving faggot!"

"I do hope that's true!" cried Brother De Prospo. "Won't that be lucky? Won't we have a grand old time in hell?"

"Sir, do you have a lawyer?" Junior asked.

"I demand trial by a papal court!" Then his crazed eyes cleared. "I remember you, Amelia," he murmured, "because you were the first. A sacrament. The best. You salted my tongue for human flesh. Now hand the torch to someone else." He paused, then cried, "Here's to Donald Turnipseed!"

"Here's to Ham Fisher," I sighed.

"Hea-vy," grunted Wilson.

"Mr. Ball," I whispered, no more conscious than a zombie, "give me a pen. Here's a pretty young girl named Becky Willett, cruelly fired from her job before witnesses by a sexist pig."

They released me. I called Joy, who sounded kind of weird, then walked the cold gray street among ghosts of the dead. A cloudless 6 A.M. No cars stirred around the Green's crust of dirty snow. Pigeons flopped near me. But I had nothing to give, and Liggett's, where I might have swiped some Cracker Jack, stood dark. One lone bum sat hooked over on a bench. Colored light bulbs, unlit, hung from department stores like frozen tears. Were the three churches open? Lonzo should have run there. In a church, fugitives can hide safe. Merry Christmas, Lonzo, cold and stiff in the morgue. And Merry Christmas to Errol Shiflet, no better than dead, passing on his diseased torch to poor Joy.

Merry Christmas, Marlene, Jenny, and Bess, who didn't deserve one day of misery, let alone these last three months, my only present. Merry Christmas, Ethel, nobody's mother, nobody's grandmother, six feet down in your pine crate. Merry Christmas, Cat Burglar and Brother DeProspo. Merry Christmas, Casey. Freezing fingers of air reached under the coat and robe to my bare body, and I stiffened.

Lord, life was messy. Wanting a warm room, I shuffled north toward my wounded house, ribs and guts bare, the secrets of its stuffing hanging out. Near the horizon, dissolving, floated a disk of moon.

My front door gaped. Fag smoke—I smelled it. A warm

breath brushed my body, and through the shattered floor-boards I heard the furnace roaring. All that had been inside another thing now lay on ruined display, drawers yanked, junk dumped on the floor. Furniture springs coiled in the dim light like snakes. Brown two-by-fours scraggled up the walls. Ethel's rags and newspapers had been gutted to their depths.

I shuffled up the plastery steps, down the bunged-up hallway to my bedroom.

"Never seen such an ungodly mess," said Joy, smoking like a fiend.

Nothing flustered me now, I was so far gone already. "You always were a pig for neatness, Joy. But how come you're starkers?"

"There isn't any other possible method," Joy said.

"How come you dropped in, Joy?" I shucked my coat.

"Just because," Joy said, like a child. "Guess I was lonely for Bobby Jo. I missed her, sister."

Things grew wavy, like inside a fishbowl. "Don't you love Errol?"

"He was part of you. But who could ever fill your place?"

"How come me?" I heard myself asking.

"Because you're free, sister," said bottomless and topless Joy. "And what we did sealed off my soul."

"You said you'd gone wild, Joy."

"To be like you, child. Keeping crime alive in the family, that's all."

"Michael's the Cat Burglar," I said, as Joy tugged off my robe.

"Michael couldn't burgle an open pit." Her hands grazed the small of my back. Hot ash from the cigarette she held brushed my bare bottom. "But we're talking about another crime. The worst one of all."

"Stop, Joy." Still, in my ruined, dead room, it was like floating in a warm garden pool to be hugged by another human. "What . . . crime?"

"Remember?" Joy asked, kissing my neck. "It was all your fault."

"Really?" I murmured. "My fault?"

184

"You knew people in the same family shouldn't do that. Your fault. Yes."

"Yes," I repeated. "All mine." I was crying. "But do I have to take all the punishment, too?"

"It's here, dear," said Joy.

The seal broke with a quiet pop, and I felt the memory fall at last out of my wound. It stood behind me in the room, where the floor creaked like a bed's rusty springs. Through tears, I saw Casey Dollarhide gaping amazed in the doorway as I seized the cocked pistol from its shell, pressed the mouth to his groin, and snapped the hammer.

CHAPTER 23

High time I brought this thing to earth and tried to sell it, though that'll probably mean faking all the names, including mine. I sure don't want to get sued, the way I'm suing Sergeant Bill Wilson. If I get even a fraction of the $75,000 for damages and harassment and God knows what all, that William Robert Ball, Jr., is trying to wangle out of the Elm City Police, I can afford to take it easy for a while. Or at least pay off those many old bills, for which the duns are threatening bloody murder. Lord knows, I deserve some rest from this hand-to-mouth hassle that's been my fate my whole life long.

The gun's clack woke me out of my trance. And there I stood, in my birthday suit, face to face, not with Daddy at all, but with a petrified Sergeant Wilson.

"You goddamned tit-show artist," he moaned. "Did it fire?"

"You again," I said.

"Trying to blow away my poor old balls . . . " With his maimed hand, he gingerly prodded himself for a wound—and with his free hand suddenly yanked the gun from me. "Guess I'm lucky," he said, pulling the pistol's top back. "Plain empty." Then he stared at Joy. "What sort of ambush did you burlesque queens set up? Goddamn prick-teasing crazies! And where'd you get this cop-killer?"

"The gun's mine!" Joy danced around, flapping her elbows. "I'll swear in court she got it from me!"

"And you? Are you the one who sent—"

"In my svelte pelt," Joy rhymed.

Mad pleasure lit Wilson's face as slowly, carefully, he pulled a yellow wad from his coat. "Answer me three questions," he said.

"Animal, vegetable, or mineral?" I said.

"Very definitely animal," Joy said.

"What brand of cigarette butt did you always leave?" Wilson asked.

"Eve," Joy replied.

"And what, ah, organ would you draw?" asked his mouth, while his eyeballs strayed from Joy's bull's eye to mine and back to Joy's.

"Pussssssy," hissed Joy.

"And what big words—?" He spaced his hands a foot apart.

"Go bust!" Joy cried out.

Now, with a crackling sound, Wilson unfurled the wadded telegram and read it to himself, lips moving silently, till finally he whispered, "He *is* a woman, for Christ's sake!"

"Haven't lived with a bad poet for nothing, you goddamn sexist," Joy said.

"Recite this," said Wilson.

"Say please, big pig."

"Please," said Sergeant Wilson.

So Joy Silverspring, with a huge crazy grin, sang out,

> "Find me where the dollar hides.
> Where the hole is blonde and big,
> Let your shift of bluecoats dig.
> That is where the pussy rides!
> Cat Burglar"

"Hey, thanks a whole damn lot, Joy," I said.

Under festoons of headlines all over the East, and in our home state of Indiana, Joy got caged in the loony ward of

University Hospital, where she set about writing her life's story, whatever she could bring herself to remember. When I visited her the first time, she announced that already a publisher had bought the rights for $10,000. Which inspired me to write all this.

Because his crimes were so terrible, and against the grain for any devout snapper, Brother DeProspo was shipped to a state hospital for the criminally insane. Probably, though, it wasn't that much worse than the Holiday Inn—whenever he stayed inside the place, which couldn't have been often. Were I not so forgiving by nature, I'd pray that a whole platoon of queers would split his backside, as Lonzo would have said. But the perverted father, or brother, or whatever, would only enjoy himself. So what was the use?

To a lady reporter who visited him for a human-interest story, he announced that he was the Holy Ghost, and did she want to have a child fathered by the Lord God? It came out in her article that as a boy of fourteen, Brother DeProspo had shot his own father through the head during a hunting accident, and his mother plain kicked him out of the house, wouldn't have a damn thing anymore to do with him, an unnatural and unforgivable thing for any mother to do, in my opinion. Within two months she married her first cousin.

DeProspo wound up in a Catholic orphanage. And in one way or another, the Mother Church had been caring for him ever since. He was but twenty-three when the Pillars of Society finally nailed him.

On New Year's Day, Michael dropped by my ruined home. "How am I supposed to handle that Axel, now that I'm all alone?" he asked.

"Love him," I said. "If he knows somebody loves him, he'll stop raising such a fit."

"He doesn't stay quiet enough to let me love Jesus," Michael said. "Besides, Wierwoo wants me to follow him to Ithaca. What will the adoption agency say when I take Axel back?"

"Sell all you own and buy them off, you mutant."

188

But I knew what to do.

"Mrs. Shiflet-Biggs, this is not even remotely tolerable!" Gorgeous George thundered a few days later. "It is the ultimate of underhanded tricks."

"Go blow, George," I said. "Consider it the Cat Burglar paying you back for what she stole."

Behind the counter, cuddling Axel while he gurgled and cooed, Mrs. Champion sighed, "Oh, the sweet, precious thing."

The girls and I cleaned house. I began with my smelly icebox, stood a trash barrel at its open door and stuffed it brim-full, pitching in covered, crud-filled dishes without bothering to see what moldered there. I wasn't up to knowing.

Trash barrels plus sixty black plastic crap bags lined our sidewalk when six days later we finished. Surveying the triumph, Marlene said, "Happy New Year, trashmen."

"Are we ever going to have our Christmas, Mother?" Jenny asked.

"I'm sicking William Robert Ball, Jr., on Sergeant Wilson," I said. "That's enough present for the whole family."

To kill the stench, I burnt incense in every room.

Homeowner's insurance paid up. By April, a pair of carpenters and I had pretty well healed the house's wounds. Well trained by Casey, I did much of the work myself. But scars still bulged. You could tell where new plaster tried to heal against the old, no matter how many coats of paint got slapped on. The furniture wasn't even worth burning. During one pilgrimage to the Salvation Army, we refurnished the whole place with well-worn stuff, nothing quite matching the rest, but clean and comforting.

Marlene learned that Jack Rader and his big toe had dropped out of Malcolm X and disappeared. I took an incomplete in my night-school lit course, but since have finished with a B-plus, more than I deserved. When I finally got around to telling my young instructor Michael's theory that God is Coincidence, he shot it down without even pausing to think. "Nonsense," he said. "In the first place, there's only a finite number of combinations experience can fall into. That's why people keep thinking the same thing at the same time. Or mention people you haven't seen since the Punic Wars, and in two minutes they call you on the phone. Or the sofa you donated to the Salvation Army surfaces ten years later and halfway around the world in a furnished villa you rented for the summer sight unseen. In the second place ... the second place—Well, does that answer your question or doesn't it?"

During my financial dealings with Bill Wilson, who would have got dumped from the force if he hadn't been lucky enough to grow famous for capturing the Cat Burglar, I heard that Billy Graham hitched a tramp steamer to Argentina, where he must be chug-a-lug champ of South America, thanks to his wondrous dead neck.

Poor Errol Shiflet, Ph.D., hitched back to Columbus, Ohio, broken like an egg. He works on the grounds crew of the Ohio State University, pronging wastepaper. He also moonlights in a tropical fish store in Graceland Shopping Center. I hope his incurable clap has somehow made him wiser, or at least more ginger.

At the end of May, my baby was born in University Hospital, where I'd once gone to have him destroyed. The minute labor started, Marlene rushed me there in Godzilla, and he came so fast they almost had to catch him in a basket, my first by natural childbirth. I don't know. Even as he tore out of me, I felt my body knitting itself back together. And lying there counting his fingers and toes glued me more solidly to the world than ever before, more even than that night on the beach after I'd robbed my Treasure House, now a gutted hulk. I returned once to shed bitter tears.

I named the baby after Daddy. Like newborn Bess, little Casey had hairy ears. When they wheeled us from delivery, I laid my Cracker Jack ring in his tiny palm.

So there you have it. Call this heap of pages what you want. For all the pain that's come my way, I can't help feeling like I got out better than I deserved, but it's only a feeling, no reason. Except the terrible sorrow that splashes over me when I let myself think at night about people lined like wrecked cars along the roadside of my past.

Then I tremble in my bed and hope that on the Last Day we will face one another with smiles of love and forgiveness.